Sept 7/07

Happy Birthday
Rebecca,

Love,

Sue
X X X
O O O

BY MARTHA BROOKS

MISTIK LAKE

MISTIK *LAKE*

MARTHA BROOKS

GROUNDWOOD BOOKS
HOUSE OF ANANSI PRESS
TORONTO   BERKELEY

Groundwood Books / House of Anansi Press
110 Spadina Avenue, Suite 801, Toronto, Ontario M5V 2K4

Published in the USA by Farrar, Straus & Giroux

We acknowledge for their financial support of our publishing program
the Canada Council for the Arts, the Government of Canada through the
Book Publishing Industry Development Program (BPIDP), the Ontario
Arts Council and the Government of Ontario through the Ontario Media
Development Corporation's Ontario Book Initiative.

ONTARIO ARTS COUNCIL
CONSEIL DES ARTS DE L'ONTARIO

Library and Archives Canada Cataloguing in Publication
Brooks, Martha
Mistik Lake / by Martha Brooks

ISBN-13: 978-0-88899-752-4
ISBN-10: 0-88899-752-3

I. Title.
PS8553.R663M58 2007   jC813'.54   C2006-905650-1

Design by Michael Solomon
Printed and bound in Canada

With all my sweet love for my husband,
Brian

And for
Jeffrey Canton

And
in memory of
Ada Brooks
1916-1995

Contents

Prologue   13

Part 1: Winter

1. Pieces of Family Life / Odella   17
2. A Secret Life / Gloria   36
3. Where We Go from Here / Odella   44
4. The Problem of Love / Gloria   57
5. From Bad to Worse / Odella   69
6. Jimmy, Again / Odella   83
7. Sunday Afternoon / Jimmy   95

Part 2: Spring

8. Family Secrets / Odella   101
9. An Unexpected Turn of Events / Jimmy   110
10. A Package from Iceland / Odella   118
11. Dazzled Again / Jimmy   125
12. A Seemingly Ordinary Man / Odella   130
13. Stars / Jimmy   133
14. Falling / Odella   139

Part 3: Summer

15. Dealing with Daniel / Gloria   163
16. Betwixt and Between / Odella   166
17. Life Beyond High School / Jimmy   173
18. Getting to Know Mr. Isfeld / Odella   176
19. The Truth Revealed / Odella   190
20. Dealing with Gerald / Gloria   193
21. Aftermath / Odella   198
22. A Birthday / Jimmy   202
23. A Final Gift from Iceland / Odella   204

Author's Note and Acknowledgements   207

Perhaps what people said was true, that any man who lived long enough would eventually realize that the way in which he was cursed was also the blessing he'd received.

— Alice Hoffman, The River King

PROLOGUE

On a stone-cold night in 1981 a carload of teenagers went joyriding out on frozen Mistik Lake. The car careened around a few ice-fishing shacks — knocking one over, eye-witnesses said — then skidded and shimmied farther out on the lake, suddenly broke through the ice and sank to the bottom.

There was one survivor — our mother, Sally. The upturned headlights showed her the way as she fought through the black freezing water. When she broke, gasping, to the surface, the weight of the water almost sucked her back down again. Somehow, she found the strength to claw her way onto the ice.

A few details point to her survival: the crazy way she was dressed — no coat in winter — and the two frost-covered windows that had been rolled down before the car left the shoreline.

It was a miracle, everyone agreed.

Mom was sixteen at the time, living on a farm near the lakeside town of Mistik Lake — 697 souls of mostly

Scottish, French, Icelandic and Ojibwe descent, and every one of them affected by the tragedy.

A community funeral was held for Tracy Lavallee, Gordon MacDonald and Peter Palsson. Mom's aunt, Gloria Thorsteinsson, flew back from Toronto to be with Mom and Grandpa Jon and Grandma Louise and show her support, as she had always had a special bond with our mother.

A year after the accident, Grandpa Jon sold the farm, owned by two generations of Thorsteinssons, and moved with Grandma Louise and our mother to Winnipeg. You'd think that there'd be no reason after that to go back to Mistik Lake, but you'd be wrong. Auntie Gloria had built a cottage overlooking the water when Mom was a little girl. Mom still loved it there, and when she married our father, Daniel, before she turned twenty, she told him that he would love it there, too.

Mistik is a Cree word meaning "wood." On hot, still summer mornings, drifting clouds of mist pass close to the surface of the lake just before the sun rises and burns them away. Then the oaks and poplars and birches that edge the water reflect back at you, all light and shadow play — everything so calm and peaceful you could almost forget the damage a lake can do.

PART 1 *WINTER*

– 1 –

PIECES OF FAMILY LIFE

ODELLA

AT NINE (1994)

Here's a family picture. It's a weekday morning at the cottage on Mistik Lake. I'm nine. We're all tangled limbs on the bed — Sarah, the ten-month-old baby, fallen asleep again on Mom's chest; five-year-old Janelle on one side of her, licking a grape Popsicle; and me on the other, my head pressed against her shoulder. Sunlight and shadows play across our skin.

"It's always the same old dream, Odella," Mom says, turning her face to me. "Just a bad dream about the accident. Grownups get bad dreams, too. It's nothing. Bad dreams can't hurt us."

"What dream?" Janelle pipes up. She sticks out her tongue, crossing her eyes with the effort of trying to see if it has turned purple yet.

I nuzzle closer to Mom's soft blonde hair, its familiar apple scent rising from the musty cottage pillows. A leafy breeze coming through the open windows grazes our bare arms and legs. I wait, hoping for some detail.

Mom says at last, "You already know far more about what happened to me than you should."

She goes silent then. Pats Sarah's back. Stares at the ceiling. We are shipwrecked on our mother's bed as we hold her and she holds us. But we are held close, all the same. Held inside her love.

AT THIRTEEN (1998)

Here's another picture: Mom walking slowly, carefully, down the little steps from the upper to the lower deck — alone, her back to me, looking out over Mistik Lake. It is a breathlessly hot August day. An orange butterfly flutters up from the trees. It soars over the water. Behind the summer screens I watch her watch it disappear before I come out onto the deck, too. Glass in hand, beaded moisture shimmering along the sides, Mom turns, then stumbles, as she greets me.

This is the summer I begin menstruating. Little Sarah has followed me into the bathroom.

"What are you doing, Odella? Why are you looking under the sink?"

"I'm looking for pads," I tell her. "I'm bleeding."

She patters off and comes back with Mom. By now I'm sitting on the can, underpants around my ankles. I'm crying.

"I can't find any pads," I say.

"Okay," Mom says, sitting down on the floor, opening the cupboard under the sink, peering inside.

"I already looked there."

She shoves her hand farther under the sink, comes out with a tattered bag of pads.

"Emergencies!" She pulls one out, hands it to me.

She sits and watches, smiling, pulling Sarah onto her knee, kissing my baby sister's unbrushed hair, wiping off a Cheerio that has stuck to the side of her face. Mom's only on her second wine cooler of the afternoon, so she's still holding herself together.

We've started to count the drinks, my sister Janelle and I.

That same summer we also begin to hide from our father just how much our mother has been drinking when he's not around. An architect, Dad spends most of his time at home in Winnipeg, working on projects for his clients at McLean Peters. He drives out to the cottage on weekends.

"What are we doing with these?" asks Janelle as we're carting empty bottles and cans in green plastic garbage bags into the woods.

"We're polluting the environment," I tell her. "When I'm old enough to drive I'll take them to recycling."

We do this every Friday afternoon before Dad arrives.

~~~

And another fragment: Janelle — skinny body squeezed into a pink bathing suit that was her favourite last summer and which she still wears even though she has two brand-new ones that fit her — hangs around listening as I say, "We were at the beach all day, Dad. Why don't *you* go and get the groceries?"

Mom, reclining on the deck, calls in to him over her shoulder, "Daniel, I thought you were going to grab something in the city."

Dad appears baffled. His clothing is rumpled. His face, even after a long day, still smells faintly of aftershave.

"Sally," he says in a slow, patient voice, "there's hardly anything in the refrigerator."

She twists around in the deck chaise. "You didn't leave me enough money!"

"I left you two hundred and fifty dollars — what happened to it?"

"It goes, Daniel," she responds, returning to her flat, dull voice. She faces the lake once again, ignoring him.

"I'll go with you, Dad," Janelle tells him eagerly.

Sarah, arms upstretched to him, dances back and forth on her bare feet.

"Daddy, Daddy, Daddy!" she chimes.

He reaches down, lifting her into his arms.

"Why don't we all go?" I say to Dad.

"You look like a bunch of ragamuffins," Dad says, smiling at all three of us, an edge to his affectionate tone.

"We're at the lake, Dad," I remind him, taking Sarah from his arms. "Just let me get this baby dressed."

"I am not a baby. I'm four," Sarah protests.

"That's right, and before we know it you'll be five," I say, as I cart her off to the bedroom to find a clean T-shirt and try to get a brush through her curls.

On our way to Isfeld's — Meats Groceries Videos and Liquor Vendor — which is Mistik Lake's only grocery store, Dad asks cautiously, "How has your mother been?"

If I tell him that Janelle and I counted seven wine coolers since noon today they'll fight all weekend. That'll be the end of our summer, we'll go back to the city and there'll be no more days at the beach. Besides, if the weekend with Dad is good, Mom sometimes cuts back.

"She's fine," I lie. "We're all fine."

He nods his head, unconvinced, but doesn't say anything else.

~~~

Sometimes, when I can't stand being the responsible one, I give Mom and Janelle and Sarah the slip. Before they can miss me or call me back to them I'm gone, into the hills that rise above Mistik Lake. Up the shouldering sides, where prairie grasses are speckled with bergamot and pasture sage as soft as feathers and wolf willow bushes and black-eyed Susan and purple blazing star. Where I can sit down and feel as if I'm sinking into the heart of the earth. In the blasting heat, far above the beach, I see Mom below sipping coolers as she watches my tanned sisters splash around in the lake.

I watch over them all — but by myself. Free of everything for an hour or so. Free to wait for copper-coloured dragonflies, rustling wings spread, to soar around me in the pale sky or, sometimes, when the magic is right, to land like angels on my bare shoulders. In the winter, back in the city, I can see those summer hills behind my closed eyes.

~~~

Every winter, our great-aunt Gloria flies to Winnipeg for her annual visit. No one ever goes to visit her in Toronto. Even though she owns the cottage at Mistik Lake, she hasn't been out there for years. It's a mystery why she chooses to see us the first two weeks of icy February.

This year, soon after she arrives, she sits on the edge of the guest bed, peeling black socks away from white flesh. Her feet are surprisingly unwrinkled, with toes painted the same colour as her fingernails. In winter — when nobody sees them!

"Will you paint my toenails?" I ask, sitting beside her.

"Now?"

"Yes," I say, pulling off my fluffy blue socks, wriggling my toes.

She laughs. "What about your sisters?"

"You can do their toes tomorrow. I want you to do mine now."

She nods and gets out her nail clippers and polish and little cotton balls and a fresh package of tissues. She has even packed a small pink towel, which she spreads, ceremonially, under my feet. She looks at me, smiles reassuringly, her thumb and index finger gripping my big toe, and I settle back to watch her clip my toenails. I love it when Auntie Gloria makes a fuss over me.

But soon Janelle discovers us and, right after that, Sarah, and then Mom, hanging around by the bedroom door, a fresh glass of white wine in her hand.

"Me, too!" says Sarah. "I want it *now*."

She snatches off her socks and clambers up onto the bed

beside me. I want to tell her to go away, but she looks so cute, her little toes wriggling.

I don't know why Mom can't see that my sisters are intruding and do something about it. Instead she stands there sipping her wine, smiling at Sarah, the baby, who all of a sudden doesn't seem so cute anymore.

"I have some old photos to show you, Auntie Gloria," Mom says. "Want me to get them?"

"I'll see them tomorrow, Sally," replies Gloria, like Mom's a little kid. "I have a lot of toes here to keep me busy. Thirty, to be precise. Or forty, of course, if you'd like yours done."

She winks at all of us, including Mom, who doesn't wink back and suddenly leaves.

"Have I offended her?" she whispers.

"I have no idea. Are you going to use two coats of polish — or three?"

Janelle, with a flat, deadened expression — the moment for her now somehow spoiled — leaves, too, and goes to her room. There she'll probably flop onto her bed, reach over the edge, grab a book off the floor and read, not showing her face until morning.

What she really wants is for somebody to go after her and coax her back to us. For once, though, that somebody isn't going to be me.

Sarah puts a thumb in her mouth, leans against me and watches, bleary-eyed, as Auntie Gloria does my toes.

~~~

Next night, around eight o'clock: Dad's been up since dawn, gone to work, come home for dinner, kissed his daughters, hugged his wife, hung around for a while and then buried himself in his study. He's brought his work home. He is always working on projects.

Mom sits at the dining-room table sorting mounds of old family photos with slow-moving hands. Small avalanches erupt. The photos slump crazily together.

"I'm so glad you've kept these photos," says Gloria, stroking Mom's back. "Look at all this history."

She lingers over a picture of herself standing with Grandpa Jon and Grandma Louise at their old farm. Grandpa Jon was Gloria's brother and it's easy to tell they were related, both blonde with the same eyes — same as Mom's — greyish green with a hint of blue, like water.

Holding the photograph by one edge, Auntie Gloria says to Mom, "This was taken just before I went to India. Remember that sari I sent you? You were what — seven?"

"Eight."

"My God — look at how young we all were."

Auntie Gloria sets it aside, smoothing one tattered edge, readjusts her reading glasses and looks over at the photograph that Mom is holding. In that one Mom's around fifteen and she's standing under Grandpa Jon's arm. They are both smiling into the camera.

"You were such a pretty girl, Sally. But you are so much prettier now."

"Am I?" Mom, who isn't drinking tonight, moves closer to her.

The picture Mom's holding makes her tear up. Of course

she loved him, I think — he was her father. But Grandpa Jon came to visit us only twice. Mom went by herself to his funeral in Vancouver.

Sarah kneels on a chair and stretches across the table to admire Auntie Gloria's emerald ring that we've all noticed but, so far, haven't mentioned.

"Are you engaged?" my baby sister asks at last.

Gloria, sixty-eight at the time, throws back her head and laughs. Then we all laugh. Mom, too, through her tears — with shy looks at Gloria.

"Darling, I'm an old maid," Gloria replies finally. She takes Sarah's plump, dimpled hands in her own and examines them. "You have five fingers on each hand! How remarkable! May I eat them?"

"Silly Auntie!" Sarah's whole body begins to shake with giggles.

Gloria sits back and smiles.

Later that night, I pick up the picture of Grandpa Jon and Mom when she was a teenager and take it to Gloria.

The flesh of her face sags slightly on seeing it again. A worry line appears at her brow.

"What's making Mom so sad?" I ask. "Is it because her father died?"

She strokes my back, like she did with Mom.

"It's complicated, honey."

Looking at Mom's picture — at the younger version of herself — I raise my eyes and ask, "So did you buy yourself that emerald ring?"

Auntie Gloria throws her balled-up socks into her open suitcase.

"It's from an admirer," she responds quietly.

This little admission fills me with happiness. It seems we're now sharing a wonderful secret. Something the rest of the family doesn't know about. It's like having a piece of Gloria all to myself.

Mom is softer for the two weeks of Gloria's visit. She still drinks, though she doesn't drink as much. But after Auntie Gloria goes back to Toronto, Mom sinks deeper into whatever it is that keeps her from us. She leaves for her class in filmmaking once a week, and doesn't get back until well after midnight.

Dad watches her, eyes dark and damp, his movements around her slow and quiet. We watch Dad watch her. Our family is not happy.

AT FIFTEEN (2000)

Our mother has taken up with Einar Bjornsson, the Icelandic filmmaker whose classes she's been attending. I go with my friend Sandy to see one of his low-budget art films called *The Last Desperate Days of Halldor Sigurdur Vigfusson and His Akureyri Thugs*, a bloody but dreary thing that we both hate.

At the reception afterwards, Einar, who is very tall, taller than Dad, keeps putting his hands on Mom and she doesn't seem to mind. I've suspected for a long time that something's going on. Some nights she gets home really late. The only good thing is that she's stopped drinking and she smiles more.

~~~

On the day that everything changes forever, I come home early from school. The last class is French, so it doesn't matter if I skip it because I'm ahead of everybody anyway, and, besides, I've got cramps.

I walk into the kitchen and see Mom bent over the sink, guzzling water from the tap. She straightens up, wiping her mouth, looking guilty, like I've caught her in the act of doing something shameful. She wipes her mouth again and hardens her gaze.

"Odella," she says, "I didn't hear you come in."

"I've got cramps," I say, "and you didn't come home last night."

I stare at her, daring her to explain herself. She used to always be at home, saying that three children were job enough.

"You really should take something for the pain," she says finally, with a wild, helpless look.

Later, as I lie on my bed, semi-comatose from menstrual pills, I hear Janelle come home with Sarah. Mom's moving around in the bedroom that she and Dad have shared for as long as I can remember. She's crying softly, opening and closing drawers. Janelle and Sarah come and lie with me on my bed, making a kind of sister sandwich, not bothering to take off their shoes or their puffy fall jackets.

Sarah's holding a picture of a red dinosaur that she's just coloured in her second-grade art class. Next thing, Dad's home, coming up the stairs. Sarah quickly covers her face with the picture. I pull it off and she stares up at me as I tell her everything will be all right.

Dad is in the hall. From there he hurries into their bedroom. There's silence for about three seconds, until we hear his bewildered voice.

"What's going on here, Sally?"

"I wanted to be gone by the time you got here," she tells him.

Dad says, "Think about this. Don't run away. What about the girls?"

"That's it," she says. "I'm sorry. I can't do this anymore. I'm dying here. I have to go, Daniel. If I don't, I'll go crazy and take everybody with me. And...I love him."

These last words hit all three of us sisters — I know Sarah and Janelle feel it, too. Mom loves him, I think. She loves Einar. Not Dad.

"Don't say that," Dad says brokenly. "For God's sake, Sally, don't do this."

Silence again. I imagine him waving his hands at her helplessly. They are both helpless people when it comes to each other. She won't be looking at him. She'll be packing underwear and sweaters and other belongings into the big duffel bag that has pull-along wheels.

Then, before we can take in what's happening, she's gone — her closet gaping.

She forgets to take her watch. It has a broad purple strap and a silver face with four turquoise dots where the 12, 3, 6 and 9 would be. You pretty much have to guess the time as the hour and minute hands sweep the dial. Sarah finds it later in the kitchen. It's too big for her but she puts it on anyway.

She climbs into my lap, pushes it up her seven-year-old arm and says, looking at the dial, "What time will it be when Mom comes home?"

Dad and I look at each other. He reaches across the table, touching Sarah's hand. "Why don't you come over here and sit with me?"

"No," she says, red-eyed, still staring at the dial. "I want to know, really."

"Really," I say, "we don't know."

This is a lie. We do know. She's just moved out — to be with the man she says she loves. She won't be back.

"Really," says Janelle, getting up from the table. "Really," she repeats, "why are you lying to her?"

"I'm not lying," I lie.

"Girls, please," says Dad.

"I'm never taking this off," says Sarah. "Not until she comes back. You're both lying. She's coming back this week-end."

"Oh, please," says Janelle. "Why don't you just grow up."

~~~

Well, Sarah is partly right. We do see Mom on the weekend. She comes in her car and takes us to our favourite book-store, where you can also have lunch.

These are the things I remember about that day. We each pick out a book, and as Mom is paying for them I am sent to the café section to find us a table. Halfway across the store I turn to look at Mom and my two sisters. Sarah presses her face against the sleeve of Mom's soft cashmere jacket as they wait in line. Janelle's standing slightly behind them, a scowl on her face as she looks towards the doors, the people coming and going.

At lunch, Sarah leaves most of her chicken-on-a-kaiser roll. Mom barely touches her pumpkin soup, while Janelle and I, who have ordered the same thing — a pasta dish — both keep stuffing it down until we are almost sick.

At the end of it all Mom drives us home. She pulls up to the house and stops the car. We all sit there for a while. Nobody says anything. It's so quiet we can hear the brown leaves skittering and swirling up our windy street.

I open the window on my side to let in some air. This seems to bring Mom to life. She draws in a quick breath and says, as if she's somehow forgotten her manners, "Well, this has been nice."

"When are you coming home?" says Sarah, sunk in the back, pushing her feet hard against the front seat.

Janelle fidgets with the power locks. *Click, click. Click, click.*

"Maybe," says Mom, turning to look at them both, "I'll see you again next week. I'll call."

Sarah tumbles over the seat and into Mom's arms.

"I don't want you to go," she says.

Mom holds her, murmuring, "I know. I know that."

Janelle gets out of the car and starts up the walk.

"Goodbye, Janelle," Mom calls after her. "I love you."

Janelle doesn't turn around.

"Okay," says Sarah. "You'll call us for sure?"

Mom nods, still watching Janelle.

Sarah clambers across me, opens the door and leaves, too.

"Don't forget the books. Your books!" Mom calls after her. Sarah doesn't hear.

"I'll take them," I say.

Mom watches until my sisters are both safely inside the house. After that she blinks as if she can't quite believe they're gone. Then she reaches into the backseat and awkwardly drags the bag of books into the front. One topples out.

Iceland in Seven Days.

"You and Einar planning a trip?" I say, feeling angry and betrayed and sick.

She's stuffing our books back in the bag, shoving her own in the side pocket of the driver's door. Turning to me again, she lays her hand on my arm, fingers my sleeve, seems about to say something, hesitates and finally whispers, "I love you."

"No, you don't," I say. "If you did, you'd stick around and take care of us."

She reaches for me, pulls me into her arms, hugging me tightly before releasing me — her eyes glistening with tears.

~~~

Two weeks after she walks out on us, Mom abandons us entirely. They were planning more than a trip, evidently, she and Einar.

"They've gone to Iceland to *live*?" I say to Dad.

"They'll be making a film over there, I guess," he tells me, mopping a tired hand over his face. His skin is grey, as if he hasn't been getting any sleep. Of course, none of us has.

"And how long will that take?"

I've picked up his letter opener. It's a brass knife with a mother-of-pearl handle. I want to stab his desk. Instead, he takes it from my hand and balances it across a pile of unopened mail.

"Odella, honestly I don't know," he says. "I just don't know. But it could be quite a while. Quite a while."

"She is coming back. Right?"

He doesn't answer. Looks at me forlornly. Putting an arm around my shoulders, he hugs me, kisses my forehead.

"I'm so sorry," he tells me. "This is not going to be easy for any of us."

~~~

Later, in bed, as all of this sinks in, I concentrate on convincing myself that maybe it's kind of like having a tooth pulled. Afterwards, there's a space that you're aware of for a while. Your tongue goes to it every morning when you are waking up — exploring where the tooth was, the little injured place where the gum is still red, pulpy and tender. Then one morning you wake up and you forget to check for the missing tooth.

It is, however, so much worse than that. Our hearts die. Then, exactly four months after Mom leaves us, Great-aunt Gloria comes for her February visit, and this time she stays for an entire month.

One Sunday near the end of her stay, Dad comes to get me out of bed.

"Gloria," he says, looking a little frantic, "is making an elaborate breakfast."

"I'm tired, Dad," I say, looking up at him staring down at me.

"It would be rude to sleep. Everyone's up."

I shut my eyes. Silence. Open them again. He's still there, hollow-eyed in the morning light. Only when my legs are actually hanging over the edge of the bed does he finally leave.

Hauling on my navy sweater, pulling it over my head like a shroud, I go to join the family.

The dining-room table gleams with polished silver. There are lit candles, a centrepiece of fruit, oranges and green apples tucked all around with bits of cedar, the good china with its blue flowers and gold edges and soft butter-yellow cloth napkins. A china frog has been brought in from the living room and now sits beside a small pitcher filled with maple syrup.

It feels like Christmas in February. We sit there slowly waking up to that feeling, looking at one another. Gloria, perfumed and graceful, pulls out her own chair, sits beside Sarah.

"Well, now," she says, helping Sarah to a pancake, centering it on her plate, "I have been thinking about the old days on the farm. Your grandpa Jon and I would sometimes go skating on Mistik Lake. We'd pick up Baldur Tomasson and his little brother, Leif, in Dad's old Packard and off we'd go. It was wonderful."

"Who is Baldur Tomasson? Is he bald?" Sarah pours a pool of syrup onto her plate.

Gloria laughs. "He was your grandpa Jon's best friend."

"Like Justine French is my best friend. And she has lots of hair. Can we go skating?"

"That's what I thought, Sarah. Out of doors is just the thing. There's nothing like it. How about the city park?" Gloria smiles expectantly at us all, her perfectly lined lips — pale coral — catching a sunbeam that trails through the window.

We choose the frozen-over duck pond at Assiniboine Park. After lending Gloria Mom's old ice skates and disentangling scarves and mitts from the shelf over the front-hall closet, we pile into the van. It's an icy Winnipeg morning, hoarfrost shimmering whitely on all the trees, an incredibly blue sky and everything so bright we squint like moles. Dad drives, shielded by sunglasses.

Once there, we step out just like an ordinary family on an ordinary Sunday, stopping by the benches to put on our skates. We have the place pretty much to ourselves. The faithful, Aunt Gloria says, are probably still in church, while we, the faithless, are out in nature. Gloria and Sarah are the first ones on the ice. Gloria skates backwards, holding on to my little sister's mittened hands as she stumbles forward, trying to catch her balance.

Soon we're all on the ice, Dad and Janelle and I making tentative loops, circling one another, going to the edges of the pond where little bushes stand frozen and frosted and glinting, before meeting up again in the centre.

Dad is the first to fall, and when Janelle and I go to rescue him, we notice he's laughing, so we fall down beside him, and then we're all laughing, tangled up in one another's arms and legs. Gloria and Sarah skate over to see what the fuss is about, looking down at us.

"Oh, Daddy," Sarah says, "you look so crazy. You all look so crazy."

She joins us, too, and after a while we all stop laughing, gazing up in amazement as Gloria skates around and around us, sunlight dusting her back where wings would sprout if she were an angel, corralling us all with her triumphant smile.

−2−

A SECRET LIFE

GLORIA

Her great-nieces back in Winnipeg aren't ready to know. But then she wonders — will she ever find the courage to tell them? One secret, and then another, and pretty soon you're living a life of secrets. And, of course, the first secret gets ensnarled with all the others. Entangled, impossibly, with other people, other lives, other lies. She can almost tease out the beginning of this lie, this secret, one summer long ago when she and Violet Isfeld both turned thirteen.

AT THIRTEEN (1943)

It was what people nowadays would refer to as a sleepover. Except that — camped overnight on the grass near the beach, the green waters of Mistik Lake rolling in, the canvas of that musty old tent flapping around them, the full moon sitting on the water, and Violet's black hair spilling over the damp pillow beside her — there was a moment in which all sense of who they were supposed to be vanished. She reached out in the darkness and found Violet's soft hand and fell in love.

AT FIFTEEN (1945)

A parade celebrating the end of World War II filled the main street of Mistik Lake — cars and trucks and tractors, banners waving, people dancing, singing, shouting. She spied Violet, moving through the crowd towards her, flushed and smiling, a pale green cardigan sliding from her bare shoulders. Gloria stood transfixed, watching as she came closer.

Suddenly Baldur Tomasson appeared at her ear, his hot breath and eager words gobbling up the moment.

"Gloria, come on! There's a party going on down at the beach!"

As he led her away she looked over her shoulder. Now Violet's smile seemed falsely bright as she turned her red lips to a fascinated boy who wouldn't stop gaping at her.

AT NINETEEN (1949)

At her brother Jon's wedding reception on the farm, she and two friends from the teachers' college up in Winnipeg filled his car with confetti. They attached old boots and tin cans to the bumper and wrote JUST MARRIED in foamed-up egg white on the back window.

Later she drove with her friends through town, yelling and honking the horn at everyone before continuing on up cemetery hill. There they surprised a few couples in cars, including Gary Fontaine with Violet Isfeld — her black hair gleaming under the sudden glare of the Packard's headlights. Gloria laughed until she screamed as Violet frantically tried to cover up all that pale exposed flesh.

Back in Winnipeg she invited a boy named Ralph in through the window of her dorm. He sweated on top of her while her dorm-mates, too shocked to react, lay as still as the stale air around them. The harder he pushed into her, the more she hated him.

For several months he showed up wherever she happened to be — before class, at the cafeteria, or standing by the elm tree under the dorm window.

"There's lover boy," said her friend Marie, who was newly engaged. "Aren't you going to put the poor guy out of his misery?"

"Just how do I do that? Do you propose murder?"

"Oh, Gloria," said Marie, rolling her pretty eyes, "you are a caution."

AT TWENTY-SEVEN (1957)

The bus from Winnipeg dropped her at the end of the road leading into Jon's farm before rolling on in the early summer dust and heat to the town of Mistik Lake.

Jon's wife, Louise, was there in the car to meet her — glowing summery cheeks, a gleeful smile as she exclaimed, "Look at you! You've turned into a glamour girl — love your hair!"

"Oh," said Gloria, flustered, unable to meet her gaze,

touching her hand to her short blonde curls. "Well, it's all right, I guess."

"And so modest," giggled Louise, who was pregnant again. No children yet, but it wasn't for lack of trying. In the eight years that she and Jon had been married, there had been four miscarriages. This was mainly why Gloria had come home for the summer. To help out and make sure this child was carried to term.

Louise hung a golden arm out the car window. "The men are haying," she said, looking over her shoulder as she backed onto a field road. "Baldur Tomasson finished up on his own land pretty quick so now he's helping Jon. We'll take them supper later."

"I'm here now," Gloria told her quietly. "I'm here to help, too."

Louise, reaching out a free hand and taking Gloria's own briefly, cautioned, "Jon doesn't want his little sister doing men's work. We'll find something for us to do in the house. Don't you worry."

To hide her disappointment, Gloria reviewed the passing fields where she had hoped to work — barley, flax, oats, wheat. If the weather cooperated, if it rained when it should, if the sun shone when it should, if there wasn't any hail, or blight, or rust, or insect infestations, Jon should have a bumper crop. There were so many ifs in farming. Not that teaching was such a great life — one lonely small town after another. That is until this year, when she'd finally landed a position in an elementary school in the city.

They pulled into the yard. Louise had planted pink petunias by the door. Other than that the house looked the same.

Later, as they made their way out to where Jon and Baldur Tomasson were working, the smell of clover and new-mown hay filling the truck, the hazy heat-filled day cooling as the sun set in the mighty west, Gloria felt a familiar tug deep in her spirit. She was glad to be home.

Baldur hadn't changed much. He was the same goofy boy she'd always known. He jumped down off the tractor, unbuttoned shirt flapping away from his body, hat flying off his head so that he could reach her before Jon did. He lifted her up, then set her down just as quickly, twirling her once before he did. Her feet left the ground again soon after, as she was held high in her big brother's arms.

Back in the kitchen, Louise said with a cheeky grin, "Baldur's carried a torch for you forever. And I know you like him. So why don't you two get hitched up?"

"Oh, I don't know," Gloria said, blushing, looking at her hands. "I just like the single life, I guess."

"Well, you be careful," Louise told her. "Don't want to end up like Violet Isfeld."

Gloria's heart began to bang around in her chest. "Oh?" she said, trying to sound casual. "And what's happened to Violet?"

Louise, snacking on a piece of bread, licked jam from her dripping fingers — licked them clean before she spoke.

"Remember that half-breed cad, Gary Fontaine? Married with six kids to Margaret Beauchamp — but all this winter he's been sneaking around with Violet. Old man Isfeld just about went crazy when he found out about it. Finally sent her to Winnipeg. Anyway, nobody's seen her since March."

Over the course of that hot, airless summer, Baldur

Tomasson proposed to Gloria under a harvest moon and she refused him; there was no rain and Jon's crops dried up; and Louise lost her fifth baby.

Then, just before Gloria left at the end of August to return to her teaching job in Winnipeg, Violet Isfeld arrived back in Mistik Lake, unmarried, a newborn baby in her arms.

AT THIRTY-SEVEN (1967)

Traffic inched along the busy Toronto street eleven storeys below. She watched it all from her office at Child and Family Services, her teaching days long behind her. She came away from the window then to reread the letter from home — an invitation to spend Christmas on the farm with Jon and Louise and their miraculous two-year-old daughter, Sally.

"I don't suppose we'll ever come to you now," Louise wrote wistfully. "It's just so expensive for the three of us to fly out there to Ontario. Farming's been pretty good these past couple of years, but as you know, it's never that good. Sally's getting to be such a big girl you won't recognize her. I've even taught her to say GLORIA! She yells it and throws her arms out wide and it's so darn cute that Jon and me just laugh ourselves silly. Please come. We miss you so much."

～～～

Sally's hair was silky and the colour of pale honey. It curled endearingly at the back of her neck. Gloria didn't have a single regret not having a man in her life, but being childless filled her with an ache and dogged her like a shadow all through the two weeks she spent back home. She made excuses to take Sally everywhere, bundled pink and warm in snowsuit, mitts and floppy knitted hat, eyes shining with cold, breath hovering with lacy delicacy on the steely air.

On the second-to-last day of her visit, they drove into town and ran into Violet Isfeld and her ten-year-old son, Gerald.

Even on the last day of December, Violet managed to look unencumbered by winter's trappings, her black hair caught in a single braid that was fluffed with snow like dandelion parachutes, her throat muffled with a rose-coloured scarf.

Gerald, upon introduction, sullenly shoved his hands into his pockets and looked at his feet.

"Well, Gloria!" Violet reached a free arm to wrap both her and Sally in a tight embrace. As if they were somehow reconnecting after a short absence, when indeed it had been years since they'd drifted their own separate ways.

"You look wonderful!" Violet gushed.

"Well, I'm fine. Just fine, thank you." Her shyness was an excruciating weight on her tongue.

"And is this your little girl? Hello, there."

Violet took Sally's mittened hand and gently shook it. Sally quickly turned her face away, then brought it back to stare in solemn fascination at Violet's snow-spangled hair.

"Oh, no, no," Gloria stammered. "This is Jon's child. I'm just, well, back here. You know. For a visit."

"Really! Me, too!"

Gloria looked at skinny Gerald who, having taken his hands from his pockets, now clutched his mother's sleeve and tried to pull her away.

"Gerald, stop that," said Violet. And then, "So, are you… living here?"

"No, no. Toronto."

"Of course," laughed Violet. "Silly me. You just told me you were only visiting. I'm in Winnipeg now. I work on Osborne Street. A little hippie dress shop. Actually, I've managed, somehow, to own it." She laughed again. "Wow. Toronto."

"Well," said Gloria. "So, it was very nice seeing you again."

She swung away with effort, her thin, black, completely inappropriate Toronto coat clinging to her in the wind. Several moments later, though, she turned around.

"If you're ever in Toronto, call me," she shouted after Violet.

But her words fell away like the snow falling around them, thick now, filling the air and obscuring even the lampposts.

– 3 –

WHERE WE GO
FROM HERE

ODELLA

The first Christmas after Mom runs away from us — just before Auntie Gloria comes to our rescue and stays for a month — Mom sends everyone presents, even Dad. Icelandic wool sweaters in perfect colours, perfect fits, perfect styles for each of us. Mine disappears inside my sweater drawer and doesn't come out again until I lend it to my friend Sandy, who spills soup on it and finally returns it several months later after her mother has washed and shrunk it. Dad never wears his. Sarah and Janelle wear theirs until April when — as if by some weird unspoken agreement — they stuff them into the used clothing bag that I've set aside for the Cystic Fibrosis recycling van.

The second Christmas is all about handmade silver jewellery. Dad, by this time, is marked off Mom's list, but I receive a stunning Thor's hammer on a chain, which I ignore until New Year's Eve. I wear it when Dad and Janelle and Sarah and I go to The Forks. It burns against my skin and at the end of the evening I give it to some girl in the washroom because she says she likes it.

In between times, Mom sends money on our birthdays. The odd time, she calls.

Just before the third Christmas, I am the one who answers.

My seventeen-year-old heart sinks at the sound of her voice.

"Oh," I say, "it's you."

"How is my girl?"

"Which one," I say coldly. "You have three."

After a long pause, "Okay, I deserved that. How are you, Odella — really?"

"I'm fine, Mom. We're all fine. How would you expect us to be?"

"Well," she responds, "you always were mature. I'm grateful for that."

Another long pause, after which she sighs and there is a little rattle against the receiver. Is she wiping her nose, her eyes?

"So," she whispers finally, "is Sarah there? Or Janelle?"

"Mom, why do you even bother? I mean, what's the point of all this?"

"Okay, I'll just go," she says, sounding sad and weary.

A big desolate hole opens up in the centre of my chest.

"They're not here just now," I say quickly. "Do you want them to call you back? I can have them call you back."

"No, no, that's fine."

Then she's gone again.

Later, Dad's in the kitchen, his hands on Sarah's shoulders as she explains to him, increasingly insistent, exactly how Mom prepared macaroni and cheese for her.

I haven't told anybody that Mom has called, but she's entered the house telepathically anyway, because Sarah, who hasn't mentioned her for weeks, is zeroing in on this one thing to obsess about.

"She always uses real butter and real cheese and the milk has to be two percent, Dad. It can't be skim."

"Sarah, honey," says Dad, "I can't go to the store just now."

"Then I'll make it," she says, "but I have to have the other milk."

"We don't have the other milk, sweetie. That's what I've been telling you."

"But she *always* makes it with the other milk."

Dad starts grimly for the fridge. "Let's just improvise."

"No, no, no," she says, slamming the fridge door just as he's beginning to open it.

Dad looks at me helplessly. "Can you go to the store, Odella?"

"I've got homework. Why can't you wait, Sarah?"

"Because I'm *hungry*," she whines.

"But there's lots of stuff in the fridge — see?"

I open the door, exposing an array of food both prepackaged as well as prepared by Dad who, as it turns out, is a better cook than Mom.

"And look, see?" I also open the freezer. "Here's some frozen pizza. I'll thaw it out for you."

"I hate it," Sarah pouts.

I have a history test coming up soon and a major English assignment is due tomorrow.

"I'll go to the store," says Dad.

"No, Dad," I tell him. "Don't. Stop giving in to her."

"You're not my mom," says Sarah, boring through my heart with icy, dagger-like accuracy.

"Well," I retort, "if you see anybody else around here who can fill her shoes better than me, then please let me goddamn know."

"*Nobody* is expecting you to do that," says Dad, looking alarmed.

"Right," I say incredulously. "Like I haven't been doing it all along."

I lift the car keys off the counter and I'm gone.

~~~

My friend Sandy brushes my hair. But in front of her mirror, with my eyes closed, I dream that I'm at Mom's dressing table — perched on a little chair, Mom moving behind me. I feel her warmth on my back as she reaches for a hair clip. I open my eyes — just for a second expecting to see those greyish-green eyes staring into mine.

Instead, Sandy's frowning at a section of hair that has fallen against my cheek.

"Your dad's a peach," she says.

"Where did *that* come from?"

"My mother."

She lifts the stray section and incorporates it into a high

ponytail. Raises her eyes to look at her own face — at her hair the same deep brunette shade as mine, at her eyes dark as my own. We look more like sisters than my sisters and I do, and we've carried on conversations this way — millions of them in front of her mirror — since we were ten years old.

"Guys are so fickle," Sandy continues. "What guy would stick around like your dad did? I hardly ever see my dad, and he only has one daughter to worry about. Your dad has three. And he's crazy about all of you! How lucky is that, Odella."

I glare at her. I am so angry that for a minute I can't speak. And then I do.

"What's your point? Your dad, unlike my mother, didn't abandon you. He didn't go to another country to make some stupid movie and then forget to come back. He lives two hours away by plane. He comes to see you. *All* the time."

When there's no response I continue recklessly, hurting the wrong person, "And he takes you out to dinner and goes shopping with you to places that bore the hell out of him."

I watch her face fall, but am unstoppable. "And when he's not doing that he's bending over backwards arranging skiing holidays so you can spend quality time together. In Banff — do I need to remind you? Where you and he are going *again* this Christmas."

After that Sandy stops speaking to me.

~~~

On that third Christmas, Mom sends matching scarves, mitts and hats. Sarah wears hers all Christmas Day in the house, and then, after we come back from the restaurant where we've had dinner, she wants to call Mom even though it is, by that time, the middle of the night in Iceland. Dad tries to reason with her. She sits on the green chair in the family room, wrapped once again in the Icelandic scarf, head bent, tears dripping onto her knees, silver clip sliding out of her hair. Janelle turns away and flips on the TV.

Finally Dad says, "Okay, you can call her."

I shake my head no. "She won't answer, Dad! We don't even know where she is!"

"Of course we do," he tells me. "She's in Reykjavik. In bed. With Einar."

I fall back on the sofa at Janelle's feet and wait for disaster to strike as he locates and then dials Mom and Einar's phone number.

Sometimes life surprises you, though. Gives you gifts you couldn't have ever imagined, even if you were asked first what you wanted.

Mom answers the phone and Sarah goes to bed with a smile on her face. I sit on the edge of the bed and lean in to kiss her forehead. She smells like Christmas chocolates and shampoo.

"She said she loves us, Odella. And she misses us. And she's coming to see us this summer."

"She said that? Those were her actual words?"

"She promised that she'll try very hard, and a promise is a promise, right?"

I kiss her again and say, "Sweet dreams, baby."

After I settle her down, I go back to be with Janelle. Dad's now sitting in his downstairs study with a glass of Scotch.

Janelle keeps looking over her shoulder into the study, where we can see Dad's brown shoe bobbing up and down in time to music.

"He's drinking in there," she hisses.

"Stop it, Janelle," I say. "He's feeling a little sad, that's all."

"So?" Her eyes open wide. "That's the very reason why he shouldn't be drinking. I'm worried about him. Aren't you?"

"He'll be fine," I tell her wearily, surfing onto Channel 27, which is just starting a Christmas movie. "Do you want to watch this?"

"Doesn't matter," she shrugs, leaning against me, her arms folded across her chest.

So we sit there together and watch a very old movie called *It's a Wonderful Life*. It's in black and white. The family is pretty normal, with a great mom and great kids even though the dad is having a terrible time with finances and is thinking about killing himself. Then he has a vision about how things would have turned out if he'd never been born, and that makes him rethink his life.

I cry continuously through the movie and Janelle keeps threatening to go to another channel.

"This is the dumbest movie I've ever seen," she says disgustedly at one point.

"It *is* dumb. But it's cathartic," I tell her, blowing my nose on a cocktail napkin.

We stare at Donna Reed, who is crying beautifully on James Stewart's shoulder. I reach for a fresh napkin. It has little angels blowing bugles, and JOY TO THE WORLD! in red script around the edges.

"You need a boyfriend," Janelle suddenly declares. "Instead of sitting here all miserable and bawling and watching this stupid movie. What about the guy you met in September at Mistik Lake? You really liked him. Why don't you call him? Have you still got his phone number in your jewellery box?"

I turn and glare at her. "Have you been *spying* on me?"

"Don't have to," she intones. "You look at it often enough."

~~~

Last September, on our last evening at Mistik Lake, I'd walked down the hill to the beach community called Pearson's Point, leaving Dad and Sarah and Janelle at the cottage finishing a game of Scrabble.

Smoke drifted over the trees from various cottage fireplaces. Across the valley a farmer burned stubble. I watched an early rising half-moon, turned my head back and suddenly he was there — as if I'd conjured him up — walking along the shoreline.

He moved towards me as if he had something important to say but there was no need to hurry. I didn't know it yet — that slow walk — how it would ruin me for other boys, as I watched him pick his way around a boulder that rested in the water, soaking his shoes, drenching his pants.

"You're Odella McLean," he said, arriving at last, as tall as a Nordic god like so many boys in town, eyes shining down into mine, colour rising like a slow tide up his tanned cheeks. "My grandfather and your grandfather were friends growing up."

"My grandfather?" I stammered.

He laughed and shrugged. "Sorry. Small town — everybody knows everybody else. Guess you don't know who I'm talking about."

"So how do you know who I am?" I said, flirting shamelessly.

He reached down, picked up a piece of shale shaped like a boomerang, drew back his arm and flung it. We watched it wobble across Mistik Lake, touching down five times before it finally fell over on its side and sank.

"Everybody knows who you are," he said finally, with an embarrassed grin.

Our family usually managed to blend in with the rest of the cottage people who shopped at Isfeld's. Easy enough — the population in the area doubled every summer. At times we were recognized by the older townspeople, but they seemed to take us in only briefly before sliding their gazes somewhere else.

So this boy was surprising. Nodding at the ground as if he'd just made up his mind about something, he then raised his eyes, looked directly into mine and said, "Here's the deal. Go out with me?"

"I beg your pardon?"

"Double bill at the drive-in," he blurted, blushing again.

"Lots of effects. Good eye candy. Hey, I'm just asking. Ever been to a drive-in in a truck?"

"No." I laughed nervously.

"Well, there you go. Ultimate country experience. Bad speakers. Bad popcorn. Bugs on the window. My grandfather's truck is the same age as me — eighteen coming up next February. Had to get that in there somehow," he added.

He paused, waiting for me to say something.

So I did. "Who did you say your grandfather is?"

"Oh — sorry! It's Baldur. Baldur Tomasson."

"My aunt Gloria used to go skating with him! They were neighbours, right — on the farm?"

He gave me a wide smile. "Small world! Actually, my grandparents sold their farm and they're in town now. I live with them. I'm Jimmy. Tomasson. Bastard child of Mara Tomasson — but that's another story. Guess I should confess running into you like this wasn't exactly an accident. Saw you today at Gerald Isfeld's store. I've been trying to figure out all summer how we could finally...meet."

"Really." I laughed again. "Are you really somebody's bastard child?" Teasing him now, stalling for time.

"Just ask people in town," he replied matter-of-factly. "Course they might not actually talk about it — small towns being what they are — all those dark little secrets."

He paused to breathe. "Have I made an ass of myself yet? Just tell me and I'll go quietly."

Of course by then we both knew he wouldn't.

I went with him to the drive-in. We didn't actually see

the movies. We didn't buy popcorn. The minute the coming attractions appeared on the screen, we turned to each other — lips, tongues, arms, hands, bodies, sparks and heat — in an over-the-top necking session that left us both surprised and breathless.

Later we drove slowly through the night with the windows rolled partly down. His grandfather's truck was truly as old as he promised it would be — complete with a bench seat and a pine air freshener shaped like a Christmas tree that dangled from the rearview mirror.

He pulled into the little parking area that fed onto our property, hidden from the cottage by pine trees and chokecherry bushes. Below us Mistik Lake was washed with stars and a thin trail of moonlight.

We were quiet now. Almost shy again.

"Can I have your phone number?" He reached over, touching my hair.

"Do you get to the city sometimes?" I answered, and stared straight ahead.

"Not very often. But you'll be back next summer, right?"

"Right," I said, disappointed. I knew then that he wouldn't call me.

He sagged over the steering wheel, looking out at the moon. "Guess that's it," he said softly.

We finally said goodbye and he drove away slowly, his headlights making spooky arcs on the pale gravel road. I walked back up to the cottage, the memory of his hands lingering on my body.

Of course, Dad was waiting up, furious.

"Where have you been? We've all been worried sick. You

went where? With who? Odella, you didn't even know that boy. *Anything* could have happened. What's gotten into you?"

When I walked into the room I shared with Janelle and started getting undressed in the dark, she rolled over in bed.

"Where did you disappear to?" she whispered.

"I didn't disappear," I snapped. "I was just out."

"Out? It's one o'clock in the morning."

"So what."

"Odella," she said, rising on her elbows, "you made Sarah really upset. Dad and I could barely calm her down. We didn't know where you'd gone."

"Well, I'm back now. So you can all stop making me feel guilty." I whipped back the covers and fell into bed. "Disaster hasn't struck. Nothing happened to me."

We lay in the dark for a while, neither of us saying anything.

At last Janelle said wistfully, "What's his name?"

I turned my face to her on the pillow. "Jimmy Tomasson. How did you know I was out with somebody?"

I could feel her smiling in the dark. "I can smell boy cologne on you."

"It's aftershave," I said.

~~~

When we got back to Winnipeg I called Sandy, who at the time was still speaking to me.

"Why didn't you get his cell or something?" she asked.

Next thing I heard her knocking pencils and pens off the

desk, dropping books and magazines and file folders onto the floor.

"There's a rural directory somewhere here in my mom's office," she muttered. "It's here. I know it's here."

"Forget it, Sandy…"

"Found it!" she said. "Here we go — Mistik Lake."

"This isn't going to work out…"

"Who am I looking for?"

So I told her his grandfather's name, Baldur Tomasson — carefully spelling it — and the next day at school she handed me Jimmy's long-distance phone number written on a small pink piece of paper, which she had cut into the shape of a heart.

"Here," she said with a giggle. "What are you going to do about it?"

"Not sure," I told her. "Thanks."

I slipped it into my pocket and later placed it in my jewellery box.

~~~

On Christmas night, after watching *It's a Wonderful Life* with Janelle, I retrieve the heart from its not-so-secret place. I tuck it into a red silk pouch with purple drawstrings. Every night after that, I sleep with it under my pillow.

−4−

THE PROBLEM OF LOVE

GLORIA

Love is an unreasonable thing. That's something else she'd like to tell her great-nieces back in Winnipeg. You can't predict who you'll fall in love with. Of course you can live a lie and not follow your heart and suffer secretly. Which is exactly how she'd handled Violet — running into her like that at Mistik Lake and just letting her disappear down the snowy street.

Until India.

October 19, 1973
Dear Aunt Gloria,
Next month I will be 8!!! Please bring me back a silk sari when you go on your trip. Peacock blue with gold on the edges would be SENSASHONAL.

XOXOX SALLY

November 21, 1973

Dearest Sally and Jon and Louise —

On the front of this postcard is a photo of the Taj Mahal. It's as beautiful as it looks! And guess what — I just ran into somebody from Mistik Lake, right here in India. It's a small world. Hope this finds you all well.

Love,
Gloria

December 29, 1973

Gloria —

Here you are. Lovely you. And me behind the camera! Did you ever think we'd bump into each other in such a far-flung place? India, indeed. Life, as they say, is stranger than fiction. Well, kiddo, burn this letter and keep the photo. Nothing incriminating there, ha ha. Except, maybe, the way I signed it. Chalk it up to exotic climes and this psychedelic world we're living in. Feeling a little strange since I got back. Promised myself I wouldn't get sentimental on you, but here I go. Have sent along a Joan Baez tape — a reissue of her greatest hits. "Black Is the Color of My True Love's Hair" might remind you of someone.

I could ask you to write back. But I know you won't. I'll never forget you.

Love always,
Violet

October 9, 1974

Dear Jon —

Thanks for biting your tongue about me buying the cottage. Also, thanks for negotiating all those lovely woodlands to go along with it! Now, of course, I'll come back to Mistik Lake and visit more often! Take care, brother dear — love to Louise and Sally and save some for yourself.

Gloria

March 2, 1981

Dear Sally —

So good to find you safe. I am deeply sorry about your accident and the loss of your friends. I can see how devastated you are, but please remember that it wasn't your fault. Accidents happen. If you need me and finally want to talk, I'm here. I mean this.

All my love,
Auntie Gloria

February 14, 1982

Dear Gloria —

It's been a year since Sally's car accident. Hasn't gotten any easier to stay in this community and look every-one in the eye. Your old flame, Baldur Tomasson, was over the other day. Thank God, he says, Sally was just a passenger. Can you imagine if she'd been the one driving? He's right on that count, bad enough as it is. She used to be such a confident daredevil of a girl. Now all she does is get mixed up with the wrong boys and run the other way when you try to talk to her about it.

Anyway, the Hutterites have been sniffing around the farm again. Hate to call it quits, but think I'll sell this time. How are you doing out there in Toronto since your big promotion? Maybe we'll come join you. Just kidding. Winnipeg's about as big a city as either Louise or I could ever stand.

Maybe this move will be good for Sally. But it's hard for us all to leave Mistik Lake. Of course there's always summer — and Sally, especially, is grateful to have your cottage to go to. Have to say I can now appreciate your wisdom in buying it.

Love,
Jon

October 4, 1984
Dear dear Auntie —

I'm the only one of my friends who isn't going back to university this fall. Everybody seems to know what they want but me. A boy that I've been friends with since we moved here from Mistik Lake, Daniel McLean (I think I told you about Daniel, he's got blond hair and very blue eyes — the bluest I've ever seen — and he's three years older than me), decided last year that he doesn't want to be an artist anymore. He switched from Fine Arts to Architecture and he's happy about it. Now, ALSO, he REALLY wants me to be his girlfriend. I'm so confused. Don't tell Mom and Dad that I sent you this letter. They're very disappointed in me right now. Of course, it seems they are always disappointed in me.

Maybe they hoped that I'd be just perfect after we moved here to Winnipeg. But I keep disappointing them. Could you come out to Manitoba sometime soon? Maybe we could go to Mistik Lake together. I missed you this summer. You never came to the cottage. I realize it's a lot to ask, but I really need to see you. Please please come. My whole life is at stake.

I love you very much,
Sally

~~~

"I'll be there a few days before Halloween," Gloria wrote back to Sally. After that she picked up the phone and called her brother.

"She wants you to go with her to the *cottage*?"

"Seems odd," she said. "Could be snowing by then."

Jon went silent.

"What's up?" she asked.

He cleared his throat. "We're at our wits' end. She got caught up with a local boy at Mistik Lake this summer. He's far too old for her — twenty-seven — and he's not good for her. Sally's a month shy of nineteen and still floundering. If you could talk some sense into her…"

~~~

At the airport Sally rushed towards her, satiny hair caught in a high ponytail.

"Let me take that," Sally offered, breaking away from a hug, snatching up Gloria's overnight bag. "This is all you brought? My things are already packed and in the car."

"Stop," Gloria said, laughing. "I haven't seen you in over a year. Can't I catch my breath and look at you, please?"

"Sure thing!"

Arms akimbo, Gloria's smart navy-and-white satchel swinging from one hand, Sally twirled in the middle of Winnipeg International Airport, her brilliant red jacket flying out behind her like a cape. She was a radiant, heart-breakingly beautiful girl, and Gloria had no doubt that she was giving her parents a run for their money. Yet wasn't that normal for beautiful girls? Even ones who had crashed through the ice?

During the two-hour drive out to Mistik Lake it started to snow.

"This won't last," Sally assured her. "We'll be fine."

By the time they arrived, the withered autumn fields were covered with snow and the lake was the colour of slate.

"I'll handle it," said Sally, adding cheerfully, "Let's stop off at Isfeld's first and get some groceries. Besides, there's somebody there I want you to meet."

It hadn't occurred to Gloria to give more than a passing thought to the local boy that Sally had got caught up with. Now, before she asked, "Is he Violet Isfeld's son — Gerald?" she knew what Sally's answer would be.

Sally clearly couldn't wait to see him. On entering the store she rushed Gloria to the back and to Gerald. First thing, on introduction, he wiped his hands on his butcher's apron and mumbled, "Guess you know my mother."

"Violet?" Gloria said calmly. "Of course. We were once…friends."

"Friends?" said Gerald, laughing nervously. He lit a cigarette, colour rising under his skin, hands trembling.

Sally's smile faded into a questioning look, first at Gloria, then back at Gerald.

He must know, Gloria thought. Well, might as well be shot for a sheep as a lamb. "How *is* your mother?"

"Do you have avocados?" Sally asked, breaking in.

"Avocados?" replied Gerald. "You mean those dark green things with the wrinkly skin?"

"We wanted one for our salad tonight."

"We got lettuce," he said, "and tomatoes. And we got green onions and cucumbers. All the normal things you'd put in a salad."

"Oh," said Sally, blushing.

"You want steak," Gerald responded, an edge to his voice, "or pork?"

"Pork chops," Gloria said, coming to Sally's rescue, "would be very nice."

Maybe, then, he didn't know.

Visions of Violet in India, however, came flooding back in the fluorescent glare of her son's store. Making more clear than ever that if she had harboured any notion of the rightness of it, just that little island of time when she actually felt alive — what was it, sixteen, seventeen days — *nobody* else was going to share that opinion.

She remembered the day eleven years earlier when she

and Violet went to the market and purchased that small blue sari for Sally. Violet also picked out cloth for herself that shimmered in red or saffron, depending on which way the sun shone. Later they went back to Gloria's hotel, which Violet had quickly moved into the day after they bumped into each other at the Taj Mahal. Violet gently pulled off all of Gloria's clothes and draped the cloth over her naked body and lay them both back on the bed. The sounds of India came through the open window. Violet kissed her and told her just to be still, that she would take care of everything. And then she did.

Better not think of it. Surprising how, after all those years, suddenly coming upon a memory of Violet made her breath catch, made her heart ache thickly.

She turned and said to Gerald, "Why don't you join us at the cabin tonight? For dinner."

"Dinner?" He looked skeptical. "You mean *supper*? You want me to come for supper?"

"Of course," Gloria responded. "I think it's time someone in the family got to know you."

Sally sagged with relief. Back in the car, she said, "Oh, thank you, Auntie. Mom and Dad don't like him. And I think he was nervous about meeting you. But he's nice, you'll see. He really is."

~~~

October snow turned to a slow chilling rain. Gloria made a salad for three and looked over at the fireplace where her niece sat, clasped hands between her knees, staring into the licking flames. Her upswept golden hair still curled tenderly at the back of her neck — as it had when she was two.

Tossing cucumber slivers on top of tomatoes, Gloria asked, "How do you feel about him, Sally?"

Sally, brushing a strand of hair from her shining face, turned and said, "I want to be with him."

Scallions as green as spring crunched beneath the blade of the knife. Gathering them into her hand, Gloria spread them on the salad. "But what are you going to do about him?"

Sally looked into the fire. "Do I have to *do* anything?"

"What about the other one...Daniel?"

"I care about Daniel, it's true. He's quite wonderful. I might even love him in a way."

"So why this? Your parents are awfully worried about you."

Sally cast her a sour look. "Are you going to start, too? Because if you are, I can't even have this conversation with you."

But suddenly she got up from the fire, came over and threw her arms around Gloria, resting her head on her shoulder.

"Don't be disappointed in me, too, Auntie. I couldn't stand it if you were. I'm so tired of making people sad. I just want to be left alone and live my life. Why can't I do that?"

"Set the table," Gloria said gently. "Your young man will be here soon."

"My young man," Sally giggled. "You're just the best. How come you never found anybody?"

Gloria responded by opening the oven door and pouring

more wine on the pork chops. It was nearing half past seven. Violet's son was almost an hour late.

And then it was very late. Gerald didn't show up. He didn't call. Sally tried calling him. There was no answer at his grandfather's where he lived. Finally, at nine o'clock when they sat down to dinner, the phone rang. Sally knocked over a chair in her eagerness to get to it before Gloria.

"But why?" she said after several seconds, turning her face away.

Gloria poured herself a glass of red wine, and one for Sally, and cut into her pork chop. She tried not to listen in on the conversation, but the phone was attached to the wall right by the table. Night washed in. Cold stars shone beyond the windows that overlooked Mistik Lake.

She consumed her wine and poured herself another as her niece, who was now crying, pleaded with Gerald.

Sally finally put down the phone. Sat heavily in her place. Gloria leaned over and lit the candle. Its windowed reflection set two flames flickering.

"I don't, as a rule, recommend drunkenness," said Gloria, "but toss back that glass I've poured you, hon, and have a bite to eat. After that I'll pour you some more. We're going to sit here until we've finished this bottle of very expensive Chianti and you've told me a little more about this man who appears to be breaking your heart."

Gerald, as it turned out, had spent the better part of his childhood being dragged back and forth between his unstable mother and his domineering grandfather.

"She was always moving around," said Sally, launching

into Gerald's history. "He'd just get started somewhere and have to get moved again. He didn't have a chance and he's so bright, he really is. And now his grandfather isn't well and Gerald is stuck in Mistik Lake managing the store and looking after him, too."

"Where is Violet in all this?"

"They don't talk to her. Even if she wanted to help out nobody would let her."

Gloria sat back, stared at the dwindling candle, picked up the bottle and poured them each the last dregs of wine.

"Should I open another?"

"God, no," said Sally.

"Well, if you don't mind, I'm going to open one for myself."

She knew, looking back on it, that she should never have opened that second bottle of wine. It didn't help matters any more than the first bottle did, and wine, of course, loosens the tongue.

The moment of confession had just slipped out. Sally curled up on the sofa, a box of tissues beside her.

"Have you ever been in love, Auntie? I mean seriously, you must have."

Gloria, buzzing with Chianti, confessed, "Once. Oh, yes. I was in love. I was so much in love."

"What was he like?"

"It wasn't a *he*, Sally." Gloria nodded her head several times before she went into the bathroom to throw up.

When she got back, Sally surprised her — snuggling up, tossing a blanket over both of them while Gloria stared miserably into the fire.

"I have never liked men." Gloria grabbed a tissue, held it over her eyes and then blew her nose.

"Well, Auntie, I'm shocked, but that's only because I *never* suspected. I guess I've been too wrapped up in my own stuff. But I have a friend who is a dyke."

Gloria began to sob.

"It's okay, really, don't be upset." Sally patted her arm consolingly. "Lots of people are. Just means that you…you like women. Sometimes, of course," she stumbled desperately on, "women like both men and women."

Gloria heaved a deep, sorrowful sigh. "Well, that's certainly Violet."

"*Violet?* Gerald's *mother?*"

~~~

On Sunday they drove silently back to the city in time for Gloria to catch her flight home to Toronto. On the plane she sat at the back between two football players. She was wearing sunglasses at eleven o'clock at night.

She had clearly made a mess of things, confessed her darkest secret to her niece — and Sally, for her part, had sworn her to secrecy over the fact that she and Gerald were not only sleeping together but would keep right on doing it.

Then, on a cool day in spring, wearing a flowing white dress that looked absolutely fetching on her, Sally delighted her parents by marrying Daniel McLean, a young man with a bright future and the only son of well-heeled parents.

-5-

FROM BAD TO WORSE

ODELLA

By February, Jimmy Tomasson's phone number, tucked inside the red silk pouch, has started to feel magical — a kind of talisman. I sleep better knowing it's under my pillow, and it produces mostly good dreams.

In this one, though, I can't move, pinned by my own dead weight, unable to open my eyes. I think, okay, maybe I'm still asleep. I'm just dreaming. Relieved that it's only a dream, I feel a letting go, and all at once I'm drifting on my back, floating near the shore on Mistik Lake. I look up as a tree suddenly releases its leaves. Swirling towards me, they are all heart-shaped, all with phone numbers, all the same one, Jimmy's number — but then, in the way of dreams, it becomes Mom's phone number in Iceland. Suddenly I am lighter than air, as if I have no body. I can be anywhere — even fly to see her if I want.

The next night we get the news.

~~~

Dad has picked up the phone. I don't pay attention at first — until something in his tone makes me stop what I'm doing.

"Wait a minute," Dad says. "She fell? Where?" Eyes wildly shifting back and forth like he's reading bad news. "I don't understand. Slow down, Einar — back up a bit."

"What?" I say, coming to him. "Who fell?"

Dad reaches out, pulls me towards him. Shocks of alarm go through me in sick little waves.

"Dad?"

Later, he tells all of us as we gather around him.

He pulls Sarah onto his lap. He reaches up to stroke Janelle's long back. I am no longer standing close enough for anyone to touch.

"They'd hiked up this mountain," Dad says slowly, as if he's trying to see it and wants us to see it, too. So that we know, we *understand*, that Mom's no longer in this world.

"They were standing on some kind of flat area. Near a waterfall — the rocks were slippery. He turned to say something to her. And she was gone — just some random, freak…"

"She's dead? Mom's *dead*?" Sarah's voice, rising hysterically.

Dad, no longer able to hold on to her, hangs his head, covers his face with his hands. Sarah runs screaming to her room. Janelle curls up like a scared animal in front of the TV. I take the family car and drive out into the night.

It's icy. I miss a stop sign, jam on the brakes. The car

skates sideways. It hits a snowbank on the other side of the intersection.

Everything stops. My hands shake. The heater whines. My breath forms a frost cloud in front of my eyes. There are no other cars. Nobody to see that this has happened. In this quiet neighbourhood almost everyone is at home having Sunday dinner — going on in a normal way.

Mom is dead. We'll never see her again. That last moment in the car when I was fifteen and she said she loved me and I told her she didn't, that's the last moment we'll ever have together. And when she phoned two months ago, and I was pissed off and didn't want to talk to her — that's the last time I'll hear her voice.

How can she no longer be in this world? How can it be?

~~~

The funeral home suggests a "Celebration of Life" service, but none of us feels like celebrating. A large bouquet of flowers sits on our dining-room table. Five shades of roses, waxy white lilies, flaming pink daisies, baby's breath, heather, cedar — and a card propped against the vase, signed from Auntie Gloria with all of her love and regrets. She hasn't been back to see us since that time two years ago when we all went skating just after Mom left for Iceland, and now she has pneumonia and is apparently too sick to come to Winnipeg.

Sarah has convinced herself that everybody she loves is now going to die.

"Pneumonia isn't fatal," Dad assures her in the car on the day that Mom's ashes arrive from Iceland.

"But Auntie Gloria's old," Sarah insists. "Don't old people die of pneumonia?"

"Sometimes, but not usually."

"Sometimes?"

"She'll be fine, sweetheart. She's not that old and she's always been very healthy."

"Why does she have it? Why does she have pneumonia *now*? She *never* comes to see us anymore."

"Sure, she does. Don't you remember? She came for an entire month."

Sarah keeps it up until we arrive at the funeral home. After that, she doesn't talk about it again. I'm sure she thinks about it, though. I'm guessing we all think about it.

~~~

"I'm sorry to hear about your mother," Miss Wainwright says after English class, her brown eyes pooling with sympathy.

"She wasn't living with us," I say.

She reaches a perfumed hand from the sleeve of a soft green sweater. "If you need to talk…"

"Thanks." I blink, cringing from her touch, walking away.

It's hard to be angry with a ghost. They don't fight back.

Sandy, catching up to me, books pressed against her chest, says, "When's the service?"

"We already had it," I say, surprised. "Same day her ashes arrived."

I look over at her shocked face.

"It was just us, " I say quickly. "Just Dad and Sarah and Janelle and me. No need for anybody else."

I start walking ahead.

"Wait!" she yells.

I look back.

"For God's sake, Odella," she says, catching up again.

"What?"

She sighs as if I just punched her in the gut. I see there are tears flowing down her face. She drops her books right in the middle of the hallway and throws her arms around me. I feel like throwing up. And then, to my horror, I know that I'm going to, sweat pouring off me, saliva filling my mouth.

"Oh, God," I say, heading for the washroom.

Sandy follows me. Comes into the cubicle with me. Strokes my back as I'm retching into the stinky white toilet basin. Stays as I sit back against the cubicle, unable to go anywhere, not knowing what to do next.

~~~

Not long after we get the news about Mom, my sisters start sleeping with me. At first it's because I hear Sarah crying in her bed, and so I get out of mine and go to her and grip her in my arms and just hold her until she's all cried out and has soaked my pyjamas with her tears.

"Come and sleep with me," I offer, and she nods her head and takes my hand as I lead her into my room.

Next thing, Janelle appears at the bedroom door, looking

like a wraith, her hair all tangled and her eyes big with sorrow.

"Come on," I tell her. "Join the party."

She runs across the room and drapes herself across my chest, heavy for such a thin person. She's got this death lock on me, and I need to hold her as much as she needs to hold me.

So then it becomes a nightly thing. We're all lonely and what we're doing seems to be helping. We even make picnics on my bed at night in the dark, with marshmallows and gummy bears and taco chips.

After about a week of this, though, I get tired, and I'm not the only one. None of us is sleeping much. I tell my sisters that they need to sleep in their own beds. They agree but are still clingy. I can't even have a shower without one or both hanging around the bathroom. I try locking the door but they pick the lock with meat skewers and come in anyway.

I tell them I'd like to shower alone. They look at me blankly as if I'm speaking in tongues.

~~~

One Saturday I'm in Sandy's mom's car driving to Polo Park shopping mall to escape my sisters and spend the next three hours helping Sandy select shoes for her hot date that night.

Sandy drops one hand from the wheel and takes hold of mine.

"You're going to get through this, you know," she says. "Starting tonight. What do you say? Trevor Greenberg is having this party. His parents are away in Japan. Come on out with Jason and me. Have a beer or two. Have some fun. You don't always have to be babysitting your family. They'll survive without you for a few hours."

Sandy's always been kind of wild, especially after her dad left when she was twelve, but for once I decide to go along with her. After all, how can it hurt?

Later that evening I get very drunk on five bottles of beer and end up in the backseat of Paul Wisherenko's dad's car with Derrick Byrnes who has been flirting with me all evening. Sandy, who is quite blasted herself, shoves her head in the back window and says, "You take her straight home, now."

"Right," says Derrick, who is also drunk and has the giggles. "Don't wait up."

"I really, really, really need to get home," I say, hauling his arm around me, enjoying the attention.

Paul, who isn't drunk, says, "Where are we going?"

"Home, I'm going home."

"Home," he grumbles. "I'm tired of being the goddamn chauffeur for everybody. Remind me not to come next time."

But he drives me home anyway.

Derrick opens his fly as we lurch along and says playfully, "Do me."

I don't know whether to laugh or throw up.

"Oh, God, please stop," I say.

The car lurches to a halt, the door swings wide open. I stagger into the cold air and distinguish myself by retching up the five beers into a snowbank.

The next morning I'm still in bed, and Derrick calls me on my cell and asks, "Want to go out next weekend?"

I remember last September with Jimmy Tomasson. The red silk pouch containing his phone number is now, not too successfully, warding off bad dreams under my pillow. I pull it out and look at it while Derrick waits for some kind of response. I finger the purple drawstrings. The pink heart hasn't seen the light of day since December. By now, I think, Jimmy Tomasson has probably taken out lots of girls in his grandfather's truck. By now he's probably pretty much forgotten me.

So I tell Derrick yes.

~~~

A few weeks later Dad suggests that we all go out as a family to a movie. Standing at the kitchen counter ready to leave, he's looking through his reading glasses at titles in the newspaper because nobody can agree on what movie to see, and I'm not planning on going anyway.

Sarah has already helped herself to a sugary snack before they are even out the door. Janelle appears in the kitchen wearing a pink top that shows a lot of cleavage. Dad glances at her, then back at the paper, looking like something has just struck the back of his head.

"Janie, won't you be cold in that top?" he says lightly. "It's twenty below zero outside."

Janelle rolls her eyes. Sarah dives into the cupboard for another cookie.

"Put that back, please, Sarah. I'll get you something at the theatre."

I'm busy at the dishwasher stacking dishes, trying not to draw attention to myself — but it doesn't work.

"Why won't you go with us?" Dad pleads. "Don't you think it would be good if we all had a night out together?"

"I've already made plans," I tell him.

Janelle walks between us on her way to get her jacket. "You don't care about us anymore," she says coldly.

"I beg your pardon! I'm just going out. Just having a little fun."

Janelle throws Dad a look and sweeps out of the kitchen.

Dad ignores her, locking eyes with me.

"You're going out with that boy again?"

"His name is Derrick, Dad."

"I hope you know what you're doing."

"What's that supposed to mean?"

Dad gives me a defeated look and leaves with his other two daughters.

For a while it's pretty much like that every weekend. After they leave I get dressed in something that makes me feel good. Derrick takes me to some party or some bar. I drink. He pays for it all.

Sometimes, during the week, he sleeps over. I let him in through the back door after midnight when everyone is in bed. He leaves before they get up in the morning. Sex with Derrick is pretty perfunctory. Not at all the way I expected it would be. But he's warm and nice to sleep with, he sometimes makes me laugh, and he smells good.

It's seven o'clock in the morning. Sarah has just been caught stuffing an incriminating note from her homeroom teacher into the bathroom wastebasket. Janelle is in bed faking another stomach ache.

Derrick has, only seconds ago, tucked his shirt into his pants, picked up his shoes and mumbled, "Sorry, Mr. McLean." He slides past my dishevelled father who stands in the upstairs hall, purple toothbrush in one hand and a crumpled piece of paper in the other.

"Good morning, Dad," I say, leaning apologetically against my bedroom door.

"Your sister Sarah is failing almost every subject," replies Dad, ignoring Derrick, focussing on our most immediate disaster.

"My God, she can't be," I say, relieved that I'm momentarily off the hook. I go over to look at the tell-all note that he holds in his trembling hand.

"How did this happen?" he says. "Wouldn't they call? How could I have missed this?"

"I don't know. I honestly thought she was doing fine. I did, Dad. Honestly. I did."

"This is just ridiculous, Odella."

"I know it is. I know that."

Now I feel sick with guilt. My baby sister has never had such terrible marks. It's a shock to see them.

"And another thing." Dad raises his eyes. "That boy. I don't like the way he treats you."

Has he known all along about Derrick's sleepovers?

"He fell asleep," I say, lying just in case. "He didn't mean to stay, Dad."

"Acting like a coward," Dad continues. "Sneaking around. A regular gutless wonder."

The whole thing shifts in my heart. I am the gutless wonder.

"You mean me," I say, stricken.

He quickly pulls me into his arms.

"Oh, Odella," he murmurs, "I don't know what I mean anymore. Do you love the guy?"

"Of course not!"

He pulls back. Gives me a Dad look. The one that says, You're better than all of this. He leaves one hand on my shoulder, looks away, sighs and looks back at me.

"So can you tell me now, please — do you have any idea, besides your mother's death — if there's something else that's up with Janelle?"

I wipe away my tears with the back of my hand.

"It's not my fault that this family is falling apart. I didn't ask Mom to abandon us! Or to *die*, for God's sake!"

Dad visibly sags. He looks ill himself. Wounded in his heart. I could bite off my own stupid tongue for the words I have just spoken to him.

I trail sorrowfully after him into Janelle's room. She's lying in the middle of her bed, pillows tossed on the floor, her clothes scattered everywhere — spilling out of drawers, trailed around the floor and tangled up in piles. Janelle used to be a neat freak.

That hits me like a shock, too.

Janelle looks wide-eyed at me, then at Dad — who suddenly sits down beside her. He leans back against the head-board.

"I'm sick, Dad." Turning her head, looking up at him. "I really am. I think I have a fever."

"We're all sick." Dad places his hand on her forehead. "Sick at heart. Sick of being sad. Sick of every damn thing. But you know what, Janie, it's sink or swim here, and that's the hard truth of it. Swimming gets my vote."

~~~

Dad enrolls Janelle in acting classes at Prairie Theatre Exchange, and places Sarah back in dance — activities they both enjoyed before Mom left us. Derrick and I go together for a little while longer, but I don't go out drinking anymore and, truthfully, I'm sick of him, too.

One night, just as I'm getting to sleep, I hear a low whistle below my bedroom window. I stagger out of bed, pull a fleece over my head and go barefoot to meet him.

As I open the door, he pushes me back inside and immediately starts kissing me. One cold hand fumbles under my pyjama top for my breast.

"Will you just quit!" I say, pulling away. "You smell of beer."

He smiles hazily and weaves in one spot in the middle of the kitchen floor.

"Thought you'd be glad to see me. But you're no fun anymore."

"Why don't you just go home."

"I'm here now. Got anything to eat?"

He goes to the refrigerator, opens the door and stands there like a big dumb jerk in the light, peering at everything, letting all the cold air out.

I decide I really am done with all this now. I'm done with him.

"Get out of here, Derrick," I tell him. "And don't come back. I mean it."

"Yeah?" He thinks about this for a minute, and then, "Okay."

He walks away. Out the door.

Next time I see him is at school with, unbelievably, his arm around Sandy.

After that I start to help Sarah with her homework, to share cooking duties with Dad, and to pull Janelle out of bed every morning when it's hard just getting up myself. I walk around all day as if I care, smile at people when I don't feel like it, act as if everything is getting better when it isn't.

~ ~ ~

Around the end of March I find a large jade-green coil-bound journal in a sale bin. The colour reminds me of summers at Mistik Lake. Inside the pages are the palest watery blue. I bring it home, open my jewellery box and take out the red silk pouch (it's been there ever since Derrick).

I remove Jimmy's heart from the pouch and smooth it before pasting it into the journal. On the same page I sketch the outline of his face — the way the moon shone on his profile after we'd been kissing in his grandfather's truck. I remember those September kisses, like sparks. So then I draw fireflies past the open truck window. The fireflies lift to the top of the page and meet a sky of stars.

On the opposite page, I sketch myself floating on my back on Mistik Lake with hundreds of leaves toppling down around me. Just like in my dream, I'm drifting, drifting lighter than air.

−6−

JIMMY, AGAIN

ODELLA

The girl's washroom, at school. I'm there by myself. It's the second week of April, two months after Mom's death. The breeze coming in through the window is cool. The shivering arms of the cottonwood just outside are full of buds but there are no leaves yet. This is Manitoba, after all. However, the snow is gone, that's a plus, and the sun is so bright I can see the gold flecks in my brown eyes as I lean in to the mirror and listen to the crows in the tree.

The washroom door suddenly swings open and in walks Sandy. We take first-period chemistry together every Friday and that's where we should be right now.

She goes into a stall, then comes out and stands beside me, washing up.

"I don't know how you feel about it," she suddenly announces to our reflections in the mirror. "About the fact that I'm seeing Derrick now."

"I'm absolutely okay with it," I say, turning to her. "After all, I'm not seeing him anymore. Is he still mad at me?"

She looks relieved. "He's never been mad at you. So you really don't mind?"

I lean against the washstand.

"Know what?" I say. "I never even liked him. I mean, not really. I can't believe I slept with him, actually."

She looks at her feet.

"We really are okay, then, you and me?"

"Absolutely," I say, and I give her a quick hug to show that I mean it. But I feel lonelier than ever as I go to class. It's not the same with Sandy and me anymore, and that's not her fault. It's me who has changed.

~ ~ ~

Later, I make dinner for the family.

Sarah rolls peas around on her plate and mutters, "I hate these. Mom always put sugar on them."

"How can you remember *that*?" says Janelle. "I think you're making it up."

Dad, who is digging into his chicken breast — and yes, it is very over-cooked and dry and stringy, and yes, he is a much better cook than me — says, "Sarah's right, Janie, your mother did put a little sugar on peas. And they tasted very good that way."

Sarah makes a face at Janelle. "I remember lots of things."

It's as if we are all on hold, waiting for Mom to walk through the door and say hi and sit down with us like she never meant to be away — a kind of temporary absence.

I look at my plate — at the peas, the chicken, the gummy potatoes — and get up from the table.

"Leave things, Dad. I'll clean up later. I've got homework."

But tonight it's even hard to tackle history notes.

A while later there is a rap on my bedroom door and Janelle appears with the phone in her hand.

"It's for you. Some boy," she says, adding, "not Derrick."

She is about to leave. I reach out and pull her back and make her sit down on the bed with me.

"Hello," I say.

"Hi," says Jimmy.

He apologizes for possibly interrupting me. I tell him, as sparks begin to hit all my secret places, that it's not a problem.

"Oh," he says, "just thought I'd call — about your mother."

"Oh that," I say. "Yes, she died."

There is a pause, in which I worry that I am breathing too quickly, that he'll hear this.

He says, "Are you okay? Did I say something wrong?"

I respond quickly, "I'm fine. Just surprised! Where are you?"

"I'm here — in Winnipeg," he says. "Are you...doing anything tonight?"

"Who was *that*?" Janelle asks after I get off the phone.

"The boy from Mistik Lake. The one you wanted me to call."

"How come your hands are shaking? Are you going to see him?"

I nod. My mouth has gone dry. My heart won't stop pounding.

"Do you want to borrow my mango-peach lip gel?"

I nod again. She rushes off and comes back with three different shades and flavours.

We sit on the edge of my bed.

"I'm meeting him in an hour," I say, lacing her fingers with mine. "Do you want to be my fashion coordinator?"

~~~

There is a place at the end of our street that sells upscale desserts and coffee that costs only slightly less than a steak at the supermarket. But nobody I know goes there and I want him all to myself.

I arrive twenty minutes before our agreed time and find, against the back wall, a table that's shadowy and has a lit candle. I'm wearing a perfume sample that Janelle gave me as a stocking stuffer and tight jeans and an orange top I'd forgotten about, but she hadn't, that I bought early last fall because the colour practically looked edible. She also found a pair of sparkly earrings that Sandy gave me three Christmases ago.

"You look very hot," Janelle said, beaming, just before she pushed me out the door.

The place has a big window right across the front, and my heart almost stops as I see him slide to a halt in his grandfather's truck. I watch him get out and wrap his coat more tightly around him against the wind that's blowing down the street. I catch a glimpse of a shirt and tie — he's so dressed up! He comes through the door, looking for me.

I raise my arm, waving it until he sees me. He smiles and saunters over. I stand up as he leans over and bump my head on his chin. We hold onto each other, laughing.

He takes off his coat and we sit down, and when he slides his hand across the table it feels natural to take it and not let go.

"So," he says, eating me up with his eyes.

"So," I say, doing the same.

The waitress comes and asks if he'd like something, and he says, not looking away from me, "Just coffee, please."

"What kind?" she asks patiently.

"Kind?" he says, tearing away his gaze, looking up at her.

"Two Colombia roast," I say, coming to his rescue.

Jimmy tells me he's here for the weekend to visit his mother.

"I see her a couple of times a year. She had me when she was pretty young. Had to leave me with my grandparents. They're great people. Love them to death. Not boring you, am I?"

I laugh, squeezing his hand. "No."

"There are fifteen D. McLeans in the Winnipeg phone book. Did you know that?"

I laugh again. "No, I guess I've never had any reason to count them."

He looks relieved and continues, "Finally found your residence number in the Yellow Pages under McLean Peters

Architects. I thought about you all winter long. Hooked up with a couple of different girls. Wish now I'd never had their phone numbers."

He blushes deeply at this last admission.

"I went around with a guy named Derrick," I blurt out. "It was pretty bad."

"Still seeing him?"

"No. He was kind of a jerk."

I lower my eyes. I don't want him to see how involved I got with Derrick. There's this awkward silence. Only when I feel brave enough do I look back at Jimmy.

He's just hanging on to my hand, which he is now looking at. This gives me courage.

"You thought about me all winter?"

Still looking at my hand, he admits, "Last summer you made my heart go crazy."

"Same!"

He raises his eyes and now I can tell that I've caught *him* off-guard. But he doesn't turn his eyes away, just keeps looking into mine and smiling until I have to drop my gaze from the heat of his.

I start blathering about Mom dying and how hard it's been for the family — just whatever falls out of my mouth — and once I start, I find I can't stop. It's a relief to say everything out loud, to talk about it.

Jimmy listens, not acting as if he'd rather be somewhere else. There's nothing in the world but us, and the table we're sitting at, and the candle that's warm between us.

After a while he breaks in and says, "She haunts you, right?"

Just like that — so simple that it stops the noise in my head.

"Yes, that's it," I respond. "I don't think any of us thought we'd never actually see her again. We still can't quite believe it happened."

I move my other hand over the candle. It's set inside a red bell-shaped holder. The light shines through my fingers. I think about the car in the lake, headlights beaming up through the water — Mom's earlier near-miss with death.

"She used to get these really vivid dreams — nightmares, really." I raise my eyes, quickly lower them again. "The famous accident. I'm sure you've heard all about it."

"It affected lots of people," he says. "I bagged groceries last summer with a woman whose sister died that night."

I release his hand, sit back.

"Odella, it wasn't your mom's fault. Listen, my uncle Karl runs the local paper at Mistik Lake and I dug up the issue where he wrote about the accident. She was just a passenger."

"And how did you find out about her dying? Was that in your uncle's paper, too?"

"Matter of fact, it was."

"An *obituary*?"

Jimmy says uncertainly, "That's a problem?"

"*We* didn't put it in there."

"Somebody did — who obviously cared about her. It was a really nice tribute. I'll send you a copy if you like."

I consider this. Who cared about her at Mistik Lake? The thought of some anonymous person writing about her makes me feel raw inside.

Jimmy changes the subject, tells me about the ice breaking up last week — big wind sweeping through the valley, sending it all down to the south end of the lake. His uncle Karl handed him a camera and told him to go take some pictures.

"I found two big chunks resting together. Sun's shining through and the ice looks alive — just beautiful! Anyway, doesn't my uncle go and put that picture on the front page of his paper. I want to write some stories for him. Been trying to convince him for two years now. He says it's a one-man operation."

"Is that what you want to do?" I say, relieved that we've found something else to talk about. "Journalism?"

"Only thing so far that makes sense to me. Don't know how I'll swing it yet, though."

The waitress brings us our coffee. It's lukewarm. Jimmy doesn't seem to notice. He sips thoughtfully, then says, "The importance of dreams is an Icelandic thing. Did you know that?"

"The importance of dreams?"

"We both have Icelandic blood, right?"

"Yes."

"So, must be in our DNA or something, that we get the dream gene. People sit around and talk about them like it's a normal thing to do — even nightmares like your mom's. They all mean something, of course."

He hesitates. Then, "My grandmother interprets my dreams all the time. I'm starting to get the hang of this stuff."

I lean forward and challenge him. "So tell me one."

"Of *mine*? Well, okay. Here's one I still think about. Happened when I was twelve years old. It's summer — in the dream — and I'm swimming underwater. For some reason I'm really scared —"

"Something terrible will happen," I say, feeling a wave of discomfort.

Jimmy reaches out and takes my hand again. "No, in this dream something's coming up underneath me. Rising up out of the water, taking me with it. Just keeps going until we break the surface. *It* — whatever it is — leaps real high over Mistik Lake. I see the whole valley from its back. This...incredible fish."

"A *fish*?"

"Big as a freaking whale. Bigger, actually. Brilliant orange — kind of like the top you're wearing, except shiny. And..."

He closes his eyes, seeing his dream again, and I am slightly jealous of the fish for grabbing his attention.

"Its scales," he continues, "have an out-of-this-world kind of shimmer. And its eye — it's like a blue lagoon. You could practically swim in it, in his eye." He opens his own eyes and leans in playfully. "In my dream I'm thinking those actual words: *blue lagoon*. So it freaks me out later when I find out that Iceland has this famous place called the Blue Lagoon. It's a natural hot pool with milky blue water — in an old volcanic lava field. People swim in it even in winter. I want to go there someday."

I shake my head, smiling now. What kind of person has dreams like this?

"Anyway, the fish says something to me..." He breaks off, then all in a rush continues, "Next day, I tell Grandma

Lilja about the dream — right up to the place where the fish spoke. She stops me. 'Don't tell me anymore,' she says. 'It's a big dream. Pay attention. That fish is bringing you a gift.'"

"A *gift?*"

He nods, sips his coffee, which by now is cold like mine.

"She gets big dreams herself. Says that's also an Icelandic thing. Awesome, you understand — in the way that they kind of…I don't know…instruct you."

I think of my own dream, the release I felt as I floated on my back on Mistik Lake — the beauty of all those leaves swirling down around me.

"So aren't you going to tell me what it said?" I ask, feeling dizzy. "Your fish?"

He's playing with my fingers. "Probably not," he says. "Do you believe in fate — stuff like that?"

"I don't know," I say, slumping over my coffee. "What if things for us — for my family — don't get any better?"

"You'll figure it out, Odella."

"It feels like we somehow need to find her again. Does that sound crazy?"

"Doesn't sound crazy at all. I'm telling you, you'll find a way."

"How do you know?"

"Because," he says, lifting my hand, "I believe you're an amazing girl."

We stay at the coffee place until they want to close for the night. Jimmy asks for the bill, winces when he sees how much two cups of coffee cost, but pays for them anyway, and leaves the waitress a nice tip. This is very classy of him. When we get into his grandfather's old truck I know that it's about time my father is introduced, properly, to a boy who is very much worth the meeting.

~ ~ ~

Dad puts down the book he's reading and stands and offers Jimmy his hand. Jimmy takes it and calls him sir, which I can tell Dad really likes.

After that I slip outside with Jimmy again. The moon, for a moment, is hazy. A fog of wet snow has just begun to settle on the newly budded elm trees.

"April in Manitoba," says Jimmy, giving me his slow smile as I walk into his open coat. He blankets it around us.

I raise my face and find his mouth and press against him, and if history can be made with a single kiss we're doing it. I swear we're melting the falling snow as it slides off our skin, our hair.

Jimmy breaks away with a gasp, taking my face in his hands. I'm actually weak in the knees. He must be feeling it, too. His forehead comes to rest against mine, steadying us.

"I don't want to mess this up, Odella," he whispers at last, "so I'm going to go now. I don't want to be just another guy."

I astonish myself, then, just stand there and let him get in the truck and drive away, not knowing when we'll see each other again.

After that I walk back into the house, say goodnight to Dad and trip going up the stairs.

He calls from the study, "Nice boy."

"Yes, Dad," I reply. "Yes, he absolutely is."

In my bedroom I collapse onto my bed. The snow has

stopped and now it's raining and the cars are splashing through the streets. I stare at the light beams moving across my ceiling, thrilled to realize that I want this boy who dreams of magical fishes and shakes me alive with the heat of his touch.

Soon after, Janelle jumps into bed with me, jamming her cold toes against my bare legs. With Sarah's radar it isn't long before she appears, too, climbing in on the other side of me.

"So, did you have a good time?" Janelle asks. "Was he as great as the last time?"

"Awesome," I say.

"I'll bet he kissed you," says Sarah.

"We melted the snow. That's how hot he is."

"Wow," she says. "That's *very* hot."

"I'm sorry I've been so crappy to you lately," says Janelle, out of the blue.

"It's not your fault," I tell her. "I've kind of been out of the country."

"What do you mean?" says Sarah. "You mean like Mom, in Iceland?"

"She means that she's been with us in body, but not in spirit. We've missed you," says Janelle.

"I don't know why we have to tell people that she's dead," says Sarah. "I don't know why we can't just tell them she's still in Iceland."

"That's the problem," Janelle says. "It feels like she still *is* there. Like she just didn't bother to come home."

"Well, I *want* her to still be in Iceland," Sarah says sadly. "Why can't we just pretend?"

I don't say anything more to them. I'm the filling in this sister sandwich. And it's great to be here again.

−7−

SUNDAY AFTERNOON

JIMMY

His mother doesn't want to let him go. Keeps talking about how tall he is and rushing off to her tiny kitchen to make him coffee or fix him macaroni and cheese that she got on sale at Payfair.

Sunday afternoon, just before he leaves, he sits her down to have a talk.

He begins gently. "I know you love me."

"How do you know that?" She looks suspicious and broken-hearted — the only woman he's ever known who can do both at the same time.

"Mom," he says, "please stop."

"How are your grandparents?"

"They're fine. You already asked me. You could call them. Find out for yourself."

"Well, I've been busy."

He puts an arm around her. "I've had a great life with them."

"I know. I know."

"I'm telling you the truth. I am, Mom."

"Oh, God." She wipes her eyes. "We had fun this weekend, didn't we?"

He gives her another hug, kisses her cheek. "Got to hit the road. It's a long drive back."

He leaves her on the sofa smoking and goes to pack up his stuff.

"Those'll kill you, Mom," he tells her at the door.

"I'm quitting, Jimmy. I already cut back to half a pack a day."

"Oh, that's a big help," he chuckles, shaking his head.

She follows him out to the truck and watches him leave. As he pulls away from her broken-down building he glances in the rearview mirror and catches a glimpse of her shivering by the entrance, looking like a cat nobody wants to let in.

The problem of his mother never goes away. She is too much with him, even when she isn't with him. The truth is, even though he loves her he's grateful she gave him up at birth. Not the most flattering thing to think about your own mother but, as Poppa says, Thoughts are cheap and they don't hurt anybody.

Another thing, here he is, going back to Mistik Lake with fifteen bucks in his pocket — hardly worth mentioning to most people, but she could use it even if she probably wouldn't have accepted it.

Still, he should have offered.

He settles back and tries to stop thinking about her as he drives through the city. Soon he turns west, passing towns spaced like dots on a vast prairie map. In a couple of hours he'll turn again into soft rolling hills before descending into the deep wide valley of Mistik Lake.

Spring has started to show — bright green along the ditches, and the sloughs are edged with burgundy-coloured willow bushes. He misses colour during the long Manitoba winter.

He thinks about Odella glowing in that orange shirt, orange like the fish in his dream. He loves her hair, it smells so good, and her skin, and the sweet, wild heat of her.

Last summer — before he got up the courage to ask her out — his arm accidentally on purpose brushed against hers in the canned-goods section at Gerald Isfeld's store. She turned her big dark eyes on him for just a moment, like she was trying to figure out if he'd be an interesting romantic experiment.

Just before Mistik Lake, the truck's ancient heater begins to work, but the late afternoon sun has come out and feels so warm he turns off the heat completely. The chill that has held Manitoba for five long months seems, at last, to be ending.

– 8 –

FAMILY SECRETS

ODELLA

So now it's the third week of April. No one has heard from Great-aunt Gloria since February, when she had pneumonia and Dad called her to tell her about Mom.

We've always understood her to be a very private person, but why not just pick up the phone and dial her number — still in Mom's handwriting in greyish-blue ink in the little ripped-up directory under the wall phone in the kitchen?

I keep thinking about Jimmy calling me an amazing girl. I don't feel amazing, not at all, but the fact that he thinks I am gives me courage.

So Monday afternoon I'm home early, hanging around by the kitchen phone. The clock on the wall says three o'clock, meaning it's four o'clock in Toronto. I grab up the phone and quickly dial Gloria's number.

Somebody else answers.

"Oh," I say.

"Who is this?"

"Odella…" I hesitate.

A cough and then, "I've got this terrible spring cold."

"Auntie Gloria, is that you?"

"It's bridge day — her turn. Glory!" she calls. "I'm putting the phone down. Just a moment…"

She goes off to find my great-aunt. I hold the phone — hear women's laughter in the background — imagine Gloria in an apartment I've never seen, holding an afternoon bridge party with a bunch of her old dolly girlfriends who are dressed up in gold jewellery and loose-fitting outfits. Gloria standing out in something completely stylish with her toenails painted.

By the time she gets to the phone, however, everything comes out differently than I'd planned.

"I know you were sick," I hear myself tell her coldly, "and couldn't come. The flowers were nice. Are you better now?"

"Oh, Odella," she utters, "I *was* in very bad shape at the time. But there's no excuse good enough for why I haven't been in touch with the family since." There is a pause before she continues, "This whole thing with your mother has been so painful. Look, this isn't the time to talk. Can I call you back later?"

I get off the phone wishing I hadn't spoken to her that way. But when she calls back a couple of hours later, the first thing she says is, "What can I do to make it up to you?"

For a minute I can't focus. Mom leaving for Iceland. Mom dying in Iceland. In her closet at home: a rose-coloured bathrobe, a dusty ancient pair of navy Birkenstock sandals, and a fairly new silk print blouse that she'd worn only a few times but that faintly smelled of her. The blouse disappeared a week after she died. I found it later, stuffed inside Sarah's pillowcase.

"Odella? Are you still there?"

I finally answer, "I was so mean to Mom when she called…"

"Oh, honey, you were probably angry," Auntie Gloria responds, all in a rush. "Why wouldn't you be? Surely she'd understand that."

"Yes, but…it was the last time…"

"The last time you talked to her?"

I hang on to the receiver, nodding my head, falling apart as a wave of grief hits me.

Gloria's voice comes again, thick with her own tears. "Life is full of regret, Odella. It really is. I wish I could tell you differently. But there it is. And I wish I could bring your mother back so she could explain herself to you. Her actions were quite — inexcusable. I say this in spite of how much I loved her. I know you did, too."

Again silence, except for her breathing. I can't even remember why I called her.

"Well," I say, "thanks, Auntie Gloria. Thanks, anyway."

I'm about to hang up when she says, "I'm…going to come for a visit."

"You are?"

"Yes. I haven't made it out to Manitoba in quite a while. I regret that, too. Talk it over with the family. Let me know when it would be a good time for all of you."

"Oh, Auntie Gloria, that would be so nice. We all miss you so much and that's the best thing you could do for us," I say, swiping at my tears with the back of my hand.

"And, Odella?"

"Yes?"

"I might bring — a friend. If that's all right with you."

"A friend! Why, yes, that's great. That would be just great."

The day improves even more. Not even five minutes later the phone rings again and it's Jimmy.

"Would it be okay if I drove into the city to see you this weekend?"

"That would be *more* than okay! So how many days is that?"

"Three!" he says with a chuckle. "If things work out I'll be there Thursday night on account of it being Easter weekend. And I'm *really* hoping I can. I'm working on it. How are you?"

"I'm okay." My lips practically kiss the receiver. "I'm absolutely good. I'm great, in fact."

Next thing, Dad's coming through the door and I'm telling him about Auntie Gloria.

"You called her? What made you do that?"

"Figured somebody had to. Guess what, she's coming for a visit! Oh, and she's bringing a friend."

He seems muddled, going through the mail, separating the bills from the junk.

"A friend? Who?"

"I didn't ask, Dad."

"A friend. Well, I guess I need to tell you something. Gloria has a partner. Her name is Kathleen. They've been together for quite a while...years, actually."

I blink several times while this sinks in. There was only that one conversation I had with her when I was thirteen, when I asked her about the emerald ring and she told me it was from an admirer. Was the ring from Kathleen?

I follow him into his study.

"Were you just not going to bother telling us that our great-aunt is a lesbian? Or that she has a partner?"

He sits in his swivel chair, throws his head back, looks at me sideways.

"This is pretty important stuff, Dad."

"Honestly? I don't think she would have felt comfortable with any of that — not until now."

He leans forward to retie his shoe, his expression hidden by the desk and the corner of the brown leather couch with its lilac wool throw. When he reappears he sits back again rubbing his hand over his chin, which is what he always does when he doesn't want to talk about something.

"Maybe she just figured it was time," he offers at last.

"Well," I say, "we need to let her know when to come. Summer gets my vote. First week of August — at Mistik Lake."

Dad's face registers a kind of alarm. "That's your birthday," he stammers. "Your eighteenth birthday."

What the hell is bothering him?

"But isn't it a good idea — a family get-together in the summer, for a change? What's wrong with it?"

"But wouldn't you rather — I don't know — be out celebrating?"

"What's wrong with Mistik Lake? Except, maybe, for the fact that Gloria never goes there and, come to think of it, why is that? After all, she owns it."

"Okay, okay, call her." He's rustling through a bunch of

papers — like he's lost something, but isn't quite sure what it is.

~~~

First I call a conference with Janelle and Sarah in my bedroom and quietly shut the door.

"What's up?" says Janelle as I join them on the bed.

"So evidently our great-aunt Gloria," I say, looking at them each in turn, "is gay."

"A *lesbian*?" says Sarah, wide-eyed.

"Evidently."

"Auntie *Gloria*?" Janelle wrinkles up her nose. "But isn't she too old for sex? I thought — "

"She's living with a woman named Kathleen," I say, "and apparently has been for years. Dad just told me. Oh, yes, and she's coming for a visit, and that's great. And, by the way, she's bringing Kathleen to meet the family."

"That's good, right?" says Sarah, looking at both Janelle and me, checking the sister barometer.

"Who is Kathleen?" Janelle says. "Are we even going to like this woman?"

"Of course we'll like her," interjects Sarah. "If Auntie Gloria likes her, then she's probably a very nice person. Does this mean Kathleen will be our aunt, too?"

"You haven't even met her yet," I caution. "This is all very new, Sarah."

"I just want to *know*! I want to know what to call her." Sarah beams at both Janelle and me. "Won't it be nice to have two aunts?"

"God, Sarah." Janelle rolls her eyes.

But we're all excited, and my sisters are close to my ear when I call Toronto.

The woman with the cold answers again, and I realize, of course, she isn't just the bridge partner.

"Kathleen? This is Odella."

"Why, yes!" she says with sudden warmth. "Gloria's great-niece."

All at once I'm saying, "Are you and Gloria free in August? I'm just wondering…is she there?"

Sarah's whining, "Why are you saying August? We didn't say anything about August."

And Janelle's saying, "Shut up, Sarah!"

"That's *months* from now!"

"Shut the hell up!"

"Hold on, I'll get her," says Kathleen over my sisters, rustling with the receiver.

I hold on for a long pause.

Gloria finally comes on the line. "Hello?"

She sounds farther away this time, somehow, as if there are years and years and houses upon houses and too many doors between us. I'm wondering what is wrong with our family that this should happen. That any of this should happen. That Mom should disappear. And that Gloria — for whatever reason beyond this secret life she felt she had to keep from us — should disappear right after Mom.

"Auntie Gloria," I say, "why don't you and Kathleen come in August? I want us all to spend some time at Mistik Lake."

I wait for her to respond. When she doesn't, I continue, "It's my eighteenth birthday then, remember?"

"Why, yes, I remember," she says, still sounding distant. "Tell Daniel — tell your father — we'll be there."

"That's wonderful, Auntie. We'll look forward to it."

When I get off the phone, Janelle stretches back on the bed, then leans on her elbows and says, "So?"

"It's settled."

"And?"

"Nothing," I say. "They're coming."

Janelle knows I'm holding something back. And I am. Gloria's got something else she's not willing to share, I feel almost certain of it.

Sarah, sitting on the edge of the bed, isn't looking at either Janelle or me. Bouncing up and down, she smiles at the carpet, at the place where I once dropped a red felt marker and it bled into the shape, almost perfectly, of a tulip.

~~~

I try phoning Jimmy back, just needing to talk to him. His grandfather answers.

"I'm sorry, he's not here right now. And who is this?"

"Odella McLean."

"Yes, yes. I knew your grandfather, Jon. He was my friend for a long, long time before he moved to the city and we didn't see him so much. You must come and visit us. I have pictures to show you."

"Pictures?"

"Yes, yes, of the old days. I'm so sorry to hear about your mother. She grew up here, you know, in this community, and we all loved her."

"You did?" I say, tears now flowing freely down my cheeks.

"Yes, yes, poor little thing. She had some very bad luck. But nobody blamed her, you know. You should come and talk to me sometime. Why don't you come some weekend?"

People in Mistik Lake had loved her. Why is it that none of us ever knew that?

~~~

Later Jimmy calls and says, "Poppa's a fast worker. Charmed you already, I see. Everything okay?" His voice swims over my thoughts. "We're on for this weekend — nothing's changed, right? I'm still working on it."

"We're absolutely on for the weekend," I assure him.

"You're sure everything's okay? You're okay?"

"Don't worry about me. I'm fine."

People in Mistik Lake had loved her. I can't get that thought out of my head. Had she loved them, too?

– 9 –

AN UNEXPECTED TURN
OF EVENTS

JIMMY

It's quite the challenge to find part-time employment in a place the size of Mistik Lake. You pump gas at the Tempo station — which he did last summer and the summer before. You can sometimes get a few days bagging groceries at Isfeld's. There's also Marvin's OK Tire across the street, a couple of local cafés, Reid's Motel up on the highway and a struggling hardware store. Nothing else between here and the larger town of Oakwood — a half-hour drive to the south.

The only other business, the *Mistik Valley Herald* — a weekly serving five towns in the area — runs columns like the "Oakwood Library News," which alerts readers to new titles while also offering recipes like Hamburger Surprise! and Dorothy's Pound Cake. However, there *are* actual stories. For two years he's been begging his uncle to let him write just one.

Unbelievably, that morning, doesn't he get a call —

Uncle Karl, back from the health centre, his leg in a cast, telling him, "Never rains but it goddamn pours. See what you can do about getting over to Gerald Isfeld's store for me. He got robbed last night."

He doesn't have to think twice about missing the school bus and cutting classes.

The shattered front window of Isfeld's. The morning sun glinting off the broken glass that's littering the sidewalk. And Uncle Karl's camera hanging around his neck.

He stands at the entrance, thinking about how best to handle the interview, until he hears, "You coming all the way inside or are you just planning on holding up the door?"

It's Gerald Isfeld in the flesh, wiping his meaty hands on a bloody pork-splattered apron. Large, dark, part Icelandic, part French and part Ojibwe, he smiles in a strained and whipped kind of way, eyes rimmed with fatigue, and continues, "If Karl's sent you to talk to me about the break-in, then let's get it done."

Jimmy follows him into the cool fluorescent light and grocery smells.

Always full of surprises, Gerald is as well the local mayor and does things his own way — like attending a sweat lodge every Sunday, which he states is his way of going to church, end of discussion, thank you very much.

"Heckuva thing," Gerald says with a twitch of his shoulders. "But we'll get through it, won't we, there, Shirl."

The checkout clerk, Shirley Lavallee. Thirty years old and the baby sister of Tracy Lavallee, who had died in Mistik Lake the night Odella's mother escaped from drowning. She's a single mother of two.

Shirley mumbles "Hi" in his direction and blushes.

"Hi," Jimmy says, keeping his smile friendly, but not too friendly.

Shirley has something of a crush on him. That's the way of a small lakeside town. Not too many faces over the long winter months so it's easy to fixate on the wrong one. He's also come to the conclusion over the past couple of years that the only way to stay out of trouble in a small town is to keep a polite distance. You have to live with people. Most of his girlfriends, including the last one, Julie Browning, have come from Oakwood, where everybody in the valley, including himself, goes to high school.

Jimmy follows Gerald's retreating back down the gleaming centre aisle of his small but prosperous store. The strings of Gerald's apron, half undone, dangle against the faded green T-shirt that encases his thick upper torso. "ISFELD'S since 1910," it says — both front and back. Like it's part of a uniform, Jimmy thinks, yet so old that there's a rip — like a wide smiling mouth — on one shoulder sleeve.

This past year Gerald fell in love, and as a result is shacked up with Connie Pelletier, a schoolteacher and single parent. Mistik Lake has its share of lonely aging bachelors and single moms, and Jimmy can't figure out why more of them, like Gerald and Connie, don't get together. Gerald, in spite of his crusty ways, likes kids and Connie's wildly jubilant bunch of sticky-faced brats seem to dote on him.

"Robbers made off with twenty cartons of cigarettes," Gerald is saying as they reach the meat counter. "And they cleaned out all the liquor." He points at Jimmy's pencil, which is now flying across the page, and adds, "They stole my clock — better write that down, too."

"Your clock?"

"The clock, Jimmy — you know, the *clock*, the one that was always there."

Sure enough, there's an empty space on the wall behind the meat counter where there used to be a clock with a sad-looking rim, a yellowing face and heavy black lettering that read, pretty much like the T-shirt: "Isfeld, Butcher and Grocer since 1910."

"Gone," says Gerald, waving his big hands.

"Maybe they thought it was an antique."

He knows even as he says it that this probably isn't true — he can't remember it ever actually telling time.

"It's a respect issue, here!" Gerald snaps. "Taking a man's private things. Taking his history. Sooner or later, though, they'll slip up. We'll get them. It's a waiting game."

Gerald glowers in a steady and expectant way until finally Jimmy tells him, "We'll print a big picture. I'll personally see that it makes the front page. I'll mention your clock."

"Good enough." Gerald smiles slightly. "Your first story, then, is it?"

"That's right." He feels a flicker of pride.

"Too bad about Karl's leg. But you're a smart kid. About time he gave you something to do."

That's also the way of a small town. They stick up for their own. If he moves to the city, as he hopes to do in the fall, he'll miss this.

Back outside, he takes a picture of the window even

though the thieves, after smashing it, decided to enter through the front door. The shattered window looks more dramatic and will probably sell more papers. If that helps Gerald, too, then it's a bonus.

~~~

Uncle Karl's leg, entombed in a large white cast and levered up on the desk, is the first thing he sees as he comes through the front door of the *Mistik Valley Herald*.

"This is so I don't get blood clots," Karl tells him sheepishly. "They gave me painkillers and told me to keep it elevated — in bed, no less. I don't know how the hell you're supposed to run a newspaper from your bed. Did you talk to Gerald?"

"I did. How come you're here? I can take care of this."

"No darn way you can — no offense, there, buddy."

"No offense taken. Want some coffee?"

"Shee-it," groans Karl. "Grab me some pills, will you? They're in my jacket over there. I don't want any coffee. Go get your story written and I'll take care of it from here."

"And just how are you going to do that?" Jimmy fumbles through the pockets of his uncle's jacket, comes up with a clear plastic vial of white pills and hands them over.

Karl cranks the lid, shoves two in his mouth, swallows and snaps the vial shut. "Look — I can barely afford to pay myself."

"So pay me whatever you can. All I need is gas money to get to Winnipeg."

"Winnipeg!" Karl explodes, then coughs. "What's in Winnipeg — besides your mother?"

"A girl. And I'm crazy about her."

Karl chuckles. "That a fact? Well, young lover, I'll think about it."

So he writes the story and Karl's pretty pleased with it although he makes lots of changes, saying how you have to stick to the facts and not stray into reportage that's sentimental. And he's promised front-page coverage with his own byline: "Jimmy Tomasson, Special to the *Herald*."

He helps out some more with this week's paper — which because of Easter weekend has to be out a day early — and after that tracks down the issue that contains the tribute about Sally McLean.

"Can I have this?" he asks on his way to his afternoon classes. "It's about my girlfriend's mother."

"What mother?"

"Mrs. McLean."

"Sally? You mean her daughter is your new heartthrob?"

"Odella — that's right. No byline here, though. Any idea who wrote the piece?"

"Why, that'd be Gerald."

"Gerald? Gerald Isfeld?"

"Why, sure," Karl says with a look of surprise. "*Somebody* had to do it. Sally was a Thorsteinsson before she married that architect — and the family meant a lot to this community at one time."

"Yes, but why Gerald?"

"Ahhh, Jimmy, you know how it is — guy was sweet on

her years ago. He just wanted somebody to do right by her memory and figured it might as well be him. Go on now, I've kept you here long enough. Don't you start skipping classes on my account."

~~~

Later he comes home and finds Grandma Lilja in the kitchen preparing *vinarterta* for the Lutheran Ladies' Spring Craft and Bake Sale. Most Icelandic women are satisfied with five or six layers. She always makes hers tower with seven — one, she claims, for each of the seven seas.

She's just assembled the cake layers with their prune filling and is spreading the frosting. He wraps his arms around her wiry body, giving her a quick hug, and reaches to drag his finger along the top of the cake.

But she is quicker — slapping his hand before he can get there. The ensuing sting makes him giggle.

"You're such a hard-ass, Gram," he teases.

"Check your language at the door, please." She resumes patting the top of the cake with the spatula. "Did you get over to Karl's?"

"Your son's doing fine. Stop worrying. I'm helping him out."

"Good for you, Jimmy. Heaven knows he could use it. He just about kills himself as it is. I had a dream that this would happen. Now, of course, it has."

Poppa appears, standing tall and white-haired in the doorway of the kitchen, a wrench in one hand, a cup of Gram's raven-coloured coffee in the other.

"So, Jimmy," he says with a proud smile, "you finally got your wish." Then, frowning at his feet, he adds, "Is he paying you?"

Poppa's truck is old, a gas-guzzler, and its days of taking extended road trips are numbered.

"Not so far. I'm just hoping for gas money."

"That a fact?" Poppa throws a teasing look at Gram. "And is driving to Winnipeg going to be a weekly event now?"

Jimmy smiles, relieved that at least it seems like the truck will be available. Then he decides to go straight back to the *Herald*. He'll work hard for Karl, harder than he's worked for anybody, and come back home and study for the chemistry test that he convinced his teacher to let him make up tomorrow morning. Somehow it'll all work out. He just has to keep pushing until it does.

"Aren't you going to eat something with us?" Grandma Lilja asks.

"Not now," he says as he's going out the door. "I'll grab something later."

He's never felt this way about any other girl. He wants to be right there with her, holding her, breathing her in. The fact is, he can't eat. Eating is the absolute last thing on his mind.

— 10 —

A PACKAGE FROM ICELAND

ODELLA

Around six o'clock on Wednesday evening a FedEx truck pulls up to our driveway. The driver has a delivery from Iceland. Einar's return address is printed boldly on the upper left-hand corner of a large shipping box. It's bulky but surprisingly light. For sure it'll have something to do with Mom. I send up a little prayer and bring it inside.

Dad turns from making a stir-fry. "What's this?"

"It's from Einar." I set the box in the middle of the kitchen floor.

"Just leave it. We'll open it after dinner."

I poke at the packing tape. "Did you *know* about this, Dad?"

"Yes." He chops hot peppers, throws them into the wok. "I asked him to send some of her things. I thought you girls should have something of her."

"I didn't know you'd talked to him again. When was all this?"

"A while back. We had a few things to discuss."

"To *discuss*?"

Dad reaches over and takes the rice off the flame.

"He's sad, Odella."

"Wild guess," I say sarcastically. "He misses Mom?"

"Of course he does! This thing has happened to *everybody*."

"I know that," I say, subdued.

Frowning, he goes back to serving the stir-fry. I'm thinking, What's going on here? Are he and Einar secretly bonding now over the phone?

"You can't always tell what's ahead," he offers out of the blue. "Nobody can. When I married your mother…" He pauses, struggles for composure. "Thing is…if you could see what's ahead — maybe you could somehow prevent it, whatever that is, from happening."

He looks so stricken that I don't push, and angle back with a gentle probe. "What was she like?"

"When?"

"When you met her."

"She was young. We met at university."

"I know. I know all that. I mean, what was she *really* like. At…her essence."

"Her essence?" The lines on his face have furrowed more deeply since Mom left us. "She was a lot like you, Odella — generous with her family, openhearted. And she had a quality that attracted people to her. She was — incandescent, actually."

"Even after the accident?"

"Yes."

"So what happened to her?"

He quickly turns away.

"I'm sorry, Dad. I didn't mean anything by that. I really didn't."

"It's okay. You want to know. I can't blame you," he says, his back still to me. "I guess, to some degree, it was my fault."

There is, it seems, no end to this grief. I could ask him why he thinks it's his fault, but I can't stand doing that to him. Maybe another time. When he feels stronger. When we all feel stronger.

~~~

Sarah, licking her fork, keeps turning around in her chair so that the box from Iceland stays in sight. Janelle pretends not to look at it, but she's up and down from the table — first to get a hair tie, next to change her socks. Finally she comes back to just sit with her hands jammed tightly between her knees.

I want to gather my sisters in my arms and stop them from being harmed in any way by the arrival of this box. Dad and I keep exchanging glances and he looks miserable. Maybe he's worried, like me, that we're all going to be disappointed.

Finally, it's time. As he picks up a paring knife and readjusts his eyeglasses I notice how odd it is — I don't know why I've never noticed this before — that he still wears his wedding band. I examine his face as, with architectural precision, he slits apart the packing tape. He is a slender man, a tall man — even a handsome man. Surely some woman somewhere would like him. It's not that I want to fix him up with someone. It's just that I worry that along with Mom he, too, has somehow died.

I get up off my chair to help him. Not that he needs assistance. I just think that maybe one of us, instead of watching, should be with him while he does this.

"Here, Dad," I say.

As soon as I say that, Janelle and Sarah leave their chairs and the whole family surrounds the box, opening flaps, lifting plastic wrapping sheets and newspaper with indecipherable Icelandic words to get at what's inside.

At the end of it all we are left with these items:

• A pair of ornate silver manicure scissors belonging to our great-great-grandmother — which came with her on a ship when she immigrated to Canada and returned with Mom to Iceland when she went to live there.

• A pair of shimmering pearl earrings that I have never seen before.

• Two long hand-painted silk scarves — one blue, one pink — which I also don't recognize.

• A satin-lined cashmere jacket in grey and blue heather with flecks of red, that Mom wore a lot around the time she left us.

• The porcelain cat that used to sit on her dresser.

• Some books, most that I don't recognize. Mom's written in a few and that calls up a whole memory of her — sitting in a chair, bare feet slung over the arm, twining a strand of pale hair around one finger. Frowning, restlessly turning pages, scrawling notes in the margins as she sips at mugs of cold tea. After she started the film classes where she met Einar, she began to read books on everything — novels, biographies of photographers, books of essays on the work of famous filmmakers.

At the bottom of the box, carefully layered in bubble wrap, we find an album of photographs — some in place, some tucked randomly. Pictures of Auntie Gloria as a teenager, Mom as a teenager, Grandpa Jon and Grandma Louise on the farm, baby pictures of my sisters and me, one of Dad who looks up from bathing Sarah. He's smiling and his shirt is wet.

From the items that Einar has sent, Janelle wants the pearl earrings and Sarah wants the cat. Dad, we can tell, wants the scissors so we give them to him and he smiles just a little at this. And I want the jacket. It's amazing to me that all four of us want different things and that there is really no need for discussion.

The minute I put on Mom's jacket, the thing I wanted most happens. It *smells* like her, it's like having her wrapped around me. The soft wool warms my arms. I hug it to my body. I want to be alone with it, with her.

They are all looking at me.

Sarah comes over and puts her arms around my neck.

"Don't cry, Odella," she whispers. "It's okay."

I wipe my eyes with Mom's sleeve and gather her into my arms and gratefully breathe in her own sweet smell.

~~~

After that we all wander around for a few hours like we've been slugged by memory. The photos are old friends, bringing smiles to Dad and Janelle and Sarah — all these images of our family history that pretty much stopped the day Mom left.

Later, in bed, I wonder where the other photos are, the recent ones. Maybe on her final day on earth she didn't take any. But for sure there'd be some of her life in Iceland, something that could maybe tell us what she cared about, what she thought about — some missing pieces of her.

I toss around for hours, not able to settle down. Finally, towards morning I drift into sleep, warm under the covers, and go to a dream place.

I'm swimming naked in warm milky blue water, aware that someone's beside me. I turn my head and it's Jimmy. His legs brush against mine, skin slipping against skin. We move in unison for a while, side by side, until he turns and gathers me all against him, hands moving over my body, his mouth finding mine.

I wake too soon. Yet I still feel him — nipple to nipple, thigh to thigh — the silkiness of everything. And seeping past the edges of dreaming I see where we were, the Blue Lagoon. I come fully awake, flip over onto my side. Rain courses down my window, drips from the eaves. I grope around for the clothes still lying in a heap from last night. My outstretched hand lights with a shock on Mom's soft jacket.

Fifteen minutes later, wide awake, *Dear Einar*, I write in

secret, not trusting anything to the Internet, composing an old-fashioned letter on Dad's fancy letterhead from his architectural firm. *Thank you for the box of items. What else do you have? Are there other photos? What did our mother do for three years in Iceland? It's important, especially for my sisters and me, to know something about her life there. Dad told me that you miss her. But so do we, her children.*

I cross out the line *What else do you have?* And sign: *Odella McLean (I am her oldest daughter).*

Later, I take Einar's letter to the post office and register it. I want him to take me seriously.

It's Thursday and I haven't heard from Jimmy since he said he was working on coming to see me. I've just spent a gazillion dollars on priority post, without giving it a second thought, and his visit probably depends on him finding enough gas money to get here. I send up another prayer. This one's for Jimmy.

— 11 —

DAZZLED AGAIN

JIMMY

In order to help out Karl, Jimmy has to work after school and in the evenings. But they make deadline and get the April 17 edition off to their customers. Finally, at five o'clock on Thursday, Karl hands him enough money to get to Winnipeg and back, generously throwing in an extra twenty bucks.

"Thank you, God!" Jimmy says, taking the money. "And you, too, Uncle Karl."

Karl laughs and sends him on his way. Back home his grandfather has already washed the truck, given it an oil change and filled the tank.

The truck, once a brilliant red, is faded now, but still gives off a slightly glorious lustre — like an old lady pumped up for a hot date.

"I knew Karl wouldn't let you down," Poppa says as Jimmy hands him the gas money.

Jimmy goes inside and calls Odella. Nobody answers, so he leaves a message, packs up his gear and heads back out the door.

Poppa, waiting by the truck, says, "I know this weekend is all about Sally McLean's beautiful young daughter, but give a thought to your mother, will you? She's still taking her medications, I hope. She can't be going off them. That just makes her crazier."

"Don't worry, I know she is. I'll check in on her."

"Good enough." Poppa reaches out, taking Jimmy's face in both hands and kisses his cheek. "Drive carefully, my boy. You are precious cargo."

Jimmy gets in and drives away. His grandfather raises his hand in a slow country wave and he raises a steady hand, too — the way he's been taught.

He can't wait to see Odella. His schizophrenic mother is another issue. Yet over the years, under difficult circumstances, he's learned ways to be a good son. That makes his grandparents proud.

The truck actually feels kind of perky. He pats the dashboard for luck. Two hours later he pulls into the outskirts of Winnipeg. Twenty minutes after that he's over the St. James Bridge, rolling down Academy Road, turning down Odella's tree-lined street. Third house from the corner, he pulls into the McLeans' driveway, parking behind the family's green van.

Before he can ring the doorbell, the door swings open wide and there she is, flanked by her sisters.

"Hello, hello, I got your message!" Odella says breathlessly.

He can already smell her perfume — something light and flowery with lemon thrown in.

"Hi."

"Jimmy — Sarah and Janelle."

The sisters smile, eyes shining. Odella walks out onto the front steps, closing the door behind her.

"They're desperate," she giggles. "I promised they'd get a chance to see you later this weekend."

"Okay," he grins, giving her his arm.

"My God, you're such a gentleman." She tucks her arm in his.

Back at the truck he realizes, looking down at the dash, that he'll soon have to put gas in the tank — what a freaking guzzler this old girl is.

Odella catches his look. "Do you want to walk to Assiniboine Park? It's only fifteen minutes away and it's such a beautiful night."

He turns off the engine, and by the time he's out of the truck she's made it around to his side. Pretty soon he's walking hand in hand with her down the sidewalk, traffic going by — walking along with this sleek and very sweet girl, the evening air rich with spring and slipping all around them.

By the river, she pulls him in front of a big elm tree. She sways against him and kisses him. After that they can't stop kissing — in front of the Pavilion, in the Leo Mol Garden, on a bench near the duck pond — his lips on her neck, her lips on his neck, their hands slipping into places that make them both whisper and laugh.

~~~

At her back door several hours later, he says, "See you tomorrow?"

"Can you come by for breakfast?"

"Count on it."

He hands her two copies of the *Herald*.

"What's this?"

"The piece I promised you about your mom. Oh, yeah, and — my first story. I'm working for my uncle's paper now."

He's proud as beneath the back-door light, she reads his name under the headline: HISTORIC GROCERY STORE, ROBBED.

"Mr. Isfeld?" She looks up at him in shock. "Was anybody hurt?"

"No, but the thieves made off with his clock. He was pretty pissed about that. By the way, he was the one who wrote the piece about your mom."

"It was Mr. *Isfeld*?"

"Yeah. Well, good night. See you in the morning."

He caresses the curve of her back and feels a thrill like fire move through his body. He can't get enough of her, and now he has to say goodnight. He watches as she turns the key in the lock and goes inside.

Then he finds an all-night gas station, drives an extra ten minutes to the outskirts of the city, turns into a field and parks. Too late to go to his mom's — she isn't expecting him.

He pulls a blanket from behind the seat, says goodnight

to the stars and thinks about Odella in her bed. After that he goes to sleep and dreams about that wondrous fish again. Immense, leaping from the water, making him feel that if he is patient and follows his heart, he will have a beautiful life.

– 12 –

A SEEMINGLY
ORDINARY MAN

ODELLA

I lie in bed, stroking my hand over his name in print —
JIMMY TOMASSON — replaying his slow, sweet kisses.
Pulling the covers over his article, pressing it like a hot
flower against my heart, I pick up the other newspaper.

This is what Mr. Isfeld wrote about my mother:

*Sally McLean, nee Thorsteinsson, died tragically in Iceland
on February 9th. She was thirty-eight years old. Mourned by
her husband, Daniel, and daughters Odella, Janelle and
Sarah. The Thorsteinssons, many of you will remember, farmed
in this community for two generations, starting with her
grandfather, Thor Thorsteinsson, and ending with her father,
Jon. Sally's life, tragically, was marked by the fatal accident on
Mistik Lake that took the lives of three others. As a woman she
was beautiful and talented and courageous. She will be missed
by many in this community who would still like to remember
her.*

I set down the paper and think about Mr. Isfeld, a seemingly ordinary man — almost gruff. But on a couple of separate occasions when we were a lot younger — he'd surprised us with little gifts.

"Girls," he'd announce with a nod as we entered his store.

He always said, "Girls," just like that — and never with a smile. Soon after, he'd disappear to the back of the store and return with items that looked as if they had been hanging around for a long time. The first time we each got a ball cap lettered with: MISTIK LAKE — WE'RE GETTING STRONGER. The second time it was LAKESIDE MUNICIPALITY badges.

Both times we looked at Mom to see what she thought of this. She turned her face away, not seeming to care, and so we took Mr. Isfeld's presents and thanked him.

After we got the badges, in the car on the way back to the cottage, Sarah said, "Why does he give us such dusty presents?"

"I'll bet he's lonely," said Janelle, adding, "and maybe he thinks his presents are nice."

"It isn't about the presents, Janelle," I said. "It's his way of saying hello. He's…eccentric."

"What does eccentric mean?" Sarah asked.

"It means," I said, "I don't know — not ordinary. Surprising."

"Quirky," Janelle offered.

"I get it!" giggled Sarah. "A man who gives dusty presents like they are flowers and drives around in a brand-new shiny truck and lets his dog put dog snot all over the windows!"

We all laughed — all except Mom who was driving, her window rolled up, leaning into it, lost in thought, not even smiling.

—13—
STARS

JIMMY

He comes out of his dream world shivering, reaching across the steering wheel to wipe fog from the glass. Sun's risen all peaches and roses with lavender-coloured clouds. It's going to be a beautiful day.

He opens the cab door, stumbles sleepily onto the prairie, stands there and takes a leak. Then he drives back to the city. At the first doughnut place he stops, uses the washroom to clean up and buys a cup of coffee. He takes it out into the chilly air where he can sit at one of their tables under the brilliant sun and watch the city come alive.

By eight o'clock he's using their pay phone to call his mother. He wakes her up. It always takes a while for her senses to kick in, so he just stands around with the phone to his ear while she does that.

Finally she says, "Are you here?"

"Yep, Mom. I'm here. Came back to see a girl."

"Will I meet her?"

"Sometime. She's great."

"Sounds serious," she says and coughs.

Then she puts down the phone and wanders off somewhere. He can hear her clattering around with her ashtrays. The sound of the toilet flushing. Water running in the kitchen sink. Dear God, he thinks, now she's going to make herself a cup of coffee. Yes, that's exactly what she's doing — while he leans against the pay phone and waits for her.

Ten minutes later she comes back and picks up the phone. He can hear her slurping away.

"Will I see you?"

"I'll be by later, Mom. I'll call first. Could be late."

"I won't go to bed," she tells him seriously.

He laughs — at them — at this whole wigged-out conversation. "I won't be *that* late."

"Who's the girl?"

"Her name's Odella. McLean. Her family has a cottage at Mistik Lake."

"Sally *Thorsteinsson's* kid?"

"That's right, Mom."

"I knew Sally. We weren't especially close. But we hung out together sometimes."

"Really."

"Don't sound so shocked, Jimmy. I wasn't always crazy. Why don't you bring her by?"

"Okay, Mom. Maybe I'll do that."

But he gets off the phone and knows that he won't. He isn't ready yet to expose Odella to this side of his life.

~~~

On Saturday night he watches Odella in the kitchen making dinner. She and her dad work like a tag team as he chops things and throws them into the salad and she tears lettuce. He puts his hand lightly on her head so he won't bump it as he swings open the cupboard door to get the salad oil. Little things that say so much about them as father and daughter, as family.

Janelle keeps changing her mind about what she wants to wear, appearing in five different outfits, each stranger than the last. She finally decides on a skinny lime-green top with dangly feathers and a pair of white pants that are so tight she can barely walk. Jimmy laughs at this last outfit, saying, "Where are you going?"

"Swimming," she answers, rolling her eyes. "At the pool."

"Swimming?" He laughs all the harder.

She seems to love this and goes back upstairs singing at full volume.

The little one, Sarah, says, "If you play Monopoly with me I'll give you the rest of my red licorice."

"Wow," he tells her with a grin. "Couldn't pass *that* one up."

Sarah is a little cheat. Though she doesn't, like some kids, try to cover it up. Whenever he calls her on stuff, she giggles and is right back at it five minutes later. Cheating, he figures, is her way of getting noticed — like Janelle in her outfits.

Odella's dad hovers around all of his girls, not saying much. At the dinner table he opens up some, asking Jimmy about his family. Avoiding the subject of his mother, Jimmy talks about working for his uncle Karl's newspaper. He can tell that Mr. McLean likes this, that it scores points with him — showing maturity and responsibility. He then mentions how he's living with his grandparents, Lilja and Baldur Tomasson.

"Baldur Tomasson," says Daniel McLean, showing a little surprise. "Did you girls know that Jimmy's grandfather used to date your aunt Gloria?"

Odella, completely surprised, says, "*Date* her? I didn't know that."

"Neither did I. Poppa's been holding out on me," Jimmy says, and feels a tug at his sleeve and turns to Sarah.

"Our auntie Gloria," she announces, "is a lesbian."

He can't help but smile. Wonders if he should — but Odella laughs just then, and after that they all do. All except Sarah.

"I don't get it," she says. "What's so funny?"

"You," says Mr. McLean, wiping his eyes, reaching over and stroking her arm. "You're a character."

"Oh," Sarah says with a happy shrug.

"I've been learning all kinds of things lately," says Odella, with a swift look at her dad.

"So I didn't know that Auntie Gloria was once straight," says Janelle.

"She wasn't," replies Mr. McLean. "I guess she just pretended to be."

"Why would she pretend?" asks Sarah.

"Well, why wouldn't she?" Janelle throws back at her. "*You* pretend all the time."

"Do not."

"Do too. Like pretending Mom isn't dead? You do that all the time."

Odella quickly gets up from the table and brings back dessert. Jimmy has two helpings even though he's full. Now she seems upset — they all do. Everybody clams up. Sarah looks crestfallen. He wants to give her a hug, but doesn't.

~~~

After dinner he and Odella make themselves scarce. He takes her to a movie. She sits in the darkness under his arm but he can feel the whole time that she isn't really there, that she's still upset about what happened at dinner.

As they're leaving the movie theatre, he offers, by way of cheering her up, "Want to take a drive out of the city and look at the stars?"

"That would be great," she says immediately. "You'd take me all the way out there just for that?"

"I'd take you — absolutely anywhere," he says, stumbling over his words, but he means it.

"Even to Iceland?" she teases.

"You want to go to Iceland with me?"

"I had a dream about us there together."

"Really," he says with a giddy flip of his heart. "Let's go right after the stars."

He drives away from the city lights. They leave the highway, head down a narrow country road and soon find a place to park — out on the prairie, the glittering star-filled night all around them.

After a while, in the darkness, Odella says, "They make you dizzy."

She turns, puts her arms around his neck. He pulls her against him as they slide down the bench seat, tongues slipping everywhere, hands slipping everywhere, too.

—14—

FALLING

ODELLA

"We have to stop now," I say, and can't quite believe myself. I've never wanted anything, anyone, so much.

Jimmy, his breath hot against my skin, lifts his face. "You want to stop?"

"Yes."

He takes this in. Slowly slides his hand away.

"Okay, okay, that's okay." He exhales, then sits up, pulls me up with him.

I button up my pants while he does the same. We settle back in the quiet of the truck, the quiet of the prairie night, and neither of us knows what to say.

The dimmer lights on the truck's dashboard illuminate his face as he turns to me again.

"Once I got to high school there were so many girls. But this is different. There's nobody like you and that's the God's truth, Odella. That's how I feel."

"I've only been with one boy," I tell him, "and that's also

the truth. I didn't even want to be with him. I wanted to be with you. Now I'm telling you to stop when I really want to be with you. Am I crazy?"

Jimmy seems about to say something, smiles instead. Lifts his hand, studies me seriously, then places it on my chest. Holds it there, light as a bird.

"I can feel your heart," he says just before he turns and starts the truck.

I sit there, still feeling his hand where it was only a second ago — the heat of it still over my heart.

The engine rumbles. We aren't moving. Jimmy's looking at me sidelong.

Finally he asks, "What's happening to us?"

"I'm not sure," I respond, lighter than I feel.

"I won't rush you, Odella. I would never do that. But I really, *really* like you. Is that okay?"

"Yeah, it's really *really* okay," I say with sudden relief, because he's said exactly the right thing. "It's absolutely definitely okay."

"Great," he says happily. "That's awesome. So what are we going to do about this summer that's coming up?"

~~~

Three days later Dad's out on the front drive washing the van and the family car. I'm cleaning out the garage, getting boxes tied up for recycling, filling garbage bags with all the useless stuff of our lives.

I put the last bag by the bin and lean against the car as he wipes it down with a towel. There's a slight slowing of the movement of the towel. He straightens, passes a hand over his forehead and looks up at the sky.

"How are you doing?" he asks.

"I'm fine, Dad. Thinking about the summer."

He opens a door, uses the damp towel to wipe the window inside. "And what are you thinking?"

"That I want to spend some time at the lake."

"Oh? How much time?"

"Maybe the whole summer."

He nods, says calmly, "All by yourself?"

"Well," I say, "you and Janelle and Sarah could come out on weekends."

"And what would you do out there all by yourself?"

"Find a job."

"Pretty tough," he says, closing the door, wiping his hands on the towel, "to find a summer job at Mistik Lake. Not much there in the way of employment."

"But if I did," I continue. "*If* I could find something — then could I go?"

He leans against the car, folds his arms across his chest, thinking.

"This boy," he says at last. "This Jimmy fellow you've been seeing. He seems like a nice boy, Odella. But you're just getting to know him. Do you really think I want you out there at the cottage trying to manage everything by yourself? I don't think you're ready for this. For any of it."

~~~

By Friday evening I am in the family car driving out to

Mistik Lake, where I've been invited for the weekend. Two hours after leaving the city, prairie flatlands give way to round wooded hills. The road weaves up through them until at last the lake appears below, rolling like a shimmering ribbon through the valley. The main road licks the shore before heading through town.

I roll down the window and smell the damp earth. It feels, in a way, like coming home. Halfway through town I take a right and follow Jimmy's instructions to the end of his street — past a red brick schoolhouse, a couple of churches, a scattering of houses.

Surrounded by a grove of aspens and oaks is his yard and the red truck. I park and get out of the car just as Jimmy appears from the back somewhere, followed by a tall white-haired man who beams and holds out a large hand.

"Odella," Jimmy says, "this is my grandfather, Baldur Tomasson."

Memories of every summer spent at Mistik Lake come flooding back as I give this old man my hand. He takes it, pulls me into his arms and clasps me in a ferocious hug.

"Welcome, welcome, welcome!" he cries. "Come in and meet Lilja. She's made you coffee! And cake!"

As I'm ushered into the house, I give a backward glance at Jimmy, who throws up his hands with a smile.

His grandmother, a tiny woman, pats my hand, beaming, too, as I take her in — her large ocean-coloured eyes.

Jimmy's grandfather stands in the middle of the kitchen and announces, "We are all Icelandic here!"

I laugh at this. It's a strange thing to say. It turns out, though, to be an introduction to what matters to him.

"I have so much to tell you! Sit, sit."

So I do.

Grandpa Baldur, at the kitchen table hoisting a mug of coffee, winks and says, "I remember your mother from the time she was just a little girl."

"You do?"

"Of course — what a tomboy! Your grandfather was always placing Band-Aids on her."

"We have a picture in our front hall," I say, "of her and Auntie Gloria skating on Mistik Lake."

"Your grandfather," he interjects, "taught her to skate by putting her on his feet."

"On his *feet*?"

"Yes, yes, we taught them all that way. Do you skate?"

"Sometimes..." I want him to go back a bit and talk about Mom and Grandpa Jon, but he's speeding ahead.

"And your *auntie Gloria*," he says, winking at Grandma Lilja, who raises her eyes to the ceiling like she's heard this one before. "Now, *there* was a *looker*." He leans back and regards me comically. "I proposed to her one summer and she turned me down! Ahhh, but that was years ago, before this one came along and knocked me on my keister. And your grandpa Jon, did you know that he wrote poetry? Of course you didn't."

As I'm smiling and shaking my head, he's rushing on. "You go to Iceland, though — like Lilja and I did in 1989 — and just about everybody there is a writer! Do you know that when the first Icelanders came to this country they were so poor all they had was lava dust in their pockets? But the books! They all brought their books. They read aloud to one another on cold winter nights. It's what kept them from going nuts!"

After that there are the family photos — all taken way over a hundred years ago in black and white — of stern unsmiling grownups, the men bearded, the women dressed in long dark skirts. In contrast, laughing children run around barefoot on the shores of massive Lake Winnipeg — a body of water reaching to the horizon — making our own Mistik Lake look like a puddle. There are fishing nets, fishing boats and heavy woollen socks flying out from clotheslines in the bitter wind. This was home to the first Icelandic settlers in Manitoba.

I feel pulled into their history, almost as if I've entered it, and I tell him so.

"This is *your* history, Odella!" he explains, pulling his chair closer to mine, stabbing an excited finger at one of the photographs. "These are your mother's people! We're all from a tiny island in the north Atlantic. Many of us became fishermen on Lake Winnipeg because it's what we did before. And we are all related, one way or another, if you go far enough back. Virtually every person you meet in Iceland will in some way be connected to you."

It's bizarre to think that Sarah and Janelle and I could somehow be related to all these people, to their ancestors in Iceland, and even to Einar. Was this part of Iceland's pull for our mother? Was that why she never came home?

"Some will be your third or fourth cousins," he continues. "All the rest, as they say in Iceland, are your ninth! They're joking, of course." He laughs. "They have genealog-

ical records that go back to the Norwegians and the Irish.
All that Viking vigour!"

"We're going to go out now, Poppa," Jimmy says, breaking in, patting his grandfather along his shoulders. And
turning to me, "Want to go for a walk?"

Grandma Lilja, having said almost nothing so far, smiles
apologetically. "Come on, Baldur," she says. "We've worn
her out and she just got here. Come — help me get that
window in the guest room unstuck."

He pushes away from the table. "I'm sorry. I've over-
whelmed you."

"But you haven't! I was enjoying it — very, very much."

"Good! So go on now. I've already taken up enough of
your time. No need to tell you everything all at once."

Jimmy and I head down his street. The evening light is
spectacular. Clouds mounding upon clouds. Silver shafts of
light gleaming from an immense sky into the valley. He puts
his arm around my shoulder, pulls me in and kisses me.

"Hi," he says.

"Hi."

"How's your ear?"

"It's great. He's great, Jimmy. I really mean that. So is
your grandmother. So — are you."

He cups my hand in the warmth of his own, puts both
our hands inside his gaping jacket pocket. We walk that way
to the lake.

"There's a boathouse up along the lakeshore that nobody
uses," he says, looking at me. "I go there sometimes."

"Oh, so this is an *invitation*."

"Yep."

"Okay, show me."

The waves rolling in are steely grey. We clamber over boulders, press past trees that crowd the shoreline — no cottages along this stretch — until, after turning a corner, there it is hidden away in a small channel — a wooden structure on stilts with water lapping underneath. After hoisting ourselves onto the pier, Jimmy lifts the latch and pulls open the boathouse door.

Inside he lights a couple of candles and the flames make shadows up the walls. The place is clammy, but I like the smell.

"Cedar," he explains. "Somebody spent a lot of money on the wood and then just abandoned it."

I run my fingers along the smooth walls. "How did *you* find it?"

"It was right after my dream about the fish." Jimmy reaches up between the rafters, pulls down a sleeping bag and continues, "I was with my best friend, Grant — he's in Calgary now — it was spring and we're going along the shoreline. And that's when we discovered it. I mean, we're kids, always snooping around, so you'd think we'd have noticed it before. Well, we keep coming back. I mean, we're curious, right? Figure somebody owns it. One day, near the end of summer, we come by and the door's wide open and nobody's around, so we climb inside. That was six years ago."

"The real owner has never been back?"

"Not to my knowledge." He looks appreciatively all around him. "I kind of feel like its caretaker."

I smile at this. And look in my own appreciation at the

sight of him pulling off his jacket and hunkering down —
muscles moving under his T-shirt — to spread the sleeping
bag on the floor.

It's big enough for two. I take off my jacket, we both kick
off our shoes and then slip down inside. It's cold at first.
Jimmy arranges the sleeping bag around us, raises his head
— sees I'm partly uncovered, pulls the bag up further.

"We came here with comic books when we were kids,"
he says, snuggling in again. "And later with various girlfriends…"

"Girlfriends. Of course. You've brought me to your bach-
elor pad. Should I be honoured?"

"Maybe I shouldn't have told you that last part," he says
with a quick laugh.

"Oh, like the double sleeping bag wasn't a dead give-
away?"

I feel a little strange — and jealous — until he puts his
hand on my heart like he did under the prairie stars. Then
suddenly he's pulling me against him and I breathe him in,
the salty smell of his sweat through his clothing. I cling to
him and feel as if I'm falling.

"Odella," he whispers, lips sparking down my neck.

"Wait, wait," I say. "Just a minute."

I struggle up, pull off my sweater, unhook my bra and
fling that off, too.

"What are you doing?" Jimmy's looking in astonishment
at my breasts.

"What do you think I'm doing?" I stare down into his
face. "I want to feel your skin, Jimmy. All of it — before I
change my mind again. Did you bring a condom?"

"Yes, but," he says, confused, "why are we rushing things? Can't we just stop for a minute?"

I lie flat again, feeling frustrated and kind of pissed off. "I thought you wanted this. Isn't that why you brought me here?"

He lies there quietly thinking, and then, "Yes, to the first part."

"And the second?"

"I don't want just to fuck you, Odella," he says in a wounded tone. "I can do that with anybody."

Silence. Now I feel wounded — and all kinds of other things I don't know what to do about. I guess he realizes this because soon there's the heat of his fingers exploring the length of my arm, finally reaching my nipples in light electric touches.

"Okay, my beauty," he whispers, like a pirate on shore leave, "let's start by taking off all these clothes."

I could remind him that that was my idea in the first place. But as we're quickly peeling everything off, tossing stuff into dark corners of the boathouse, I just want to feel him, skin to skin, all against me. I figure it'll be wonderful.

And it is.

~~~

The bed I sleep on has been made up with soft flannel sheets. Later that night, as I sink down between them, I think that they smell like summer, like the real thing — not just some chemical laundry product — and decide that the scent is a combination of all the wild plants that grow on the hill above my family's cottage. That's the last thing I think.

Next I smell coffee and it's morning and I've gone through the whole night with the stars and the moon shifting around in the sky, not waking up once.

I get dressed and go to the kitchen, where Grandma Lilja greets me with a welcoming smile.

"There she is. Did you sleep well?"

"Yes — the sheets smelled amazing."

"Lavender — from my garden. Seems a shame to waste it, so I always tie up little bundles and put them with the fresh linen."

She begins to move around her kitchen — silently, like a ship with sails. I can see the ancestors in her face. I like watching her.

"Eggs?" she asks.

"What?"

"How many?"

"Oh, none, thank you."

"I'll make you one, anyway. All that activity with my grandson will have given you an appetite."

I feel myself blushing and I want to sink under the table. I can't believe she'd say such a thing!

She whisks an egg with a fork, then drops it sizzling into the pan.

"Young people today," she adds, poking at the egg, "think that they are deceiving us old ones — that we've never felt those things. Or done those things. But of course we have! Passion isn't only for the young."

She slips my egg onto a plate, sets that in front of me.

"Eat it while it's hot. Of course, love," she continues somewhat shyly, "can be a complicated thing."

I'm finally able to meet her steady, ship-like gaze. "What should it feel like? If…it happens?"

"I can only tell you how it felt for me when I met Baldur."

She takes out a chair and sits beside me. Sips her coffee. Demurely sets it down. Picks up a basket of muffins from the middle of the table, offering them to me. I take one and bite into it, the warm, spicy sweetness filling my mouth.

Tracing one finger over the tablecloth as if she's drawing a map, Grandma Lilja answers at last, "It feels like coming home."

"Coming home?"

"Yes."

In the quiet of her kitchen, I think about home. My idea of home isn't like this one — so full of comfort mixed with history.

"I know all about your mother leaving you," Grandma Lilja says, putting her arm around me, clasping me tight — a hard grip for such a small woman. "You need to forgive her. Don't you think?"

The muffin I've been nibbling sticks in my throat.

The clock in her kitchen ticks noisily. A gust of wind blows up and shakes her window. She is wearing a thick pink cardigan. One of the buttons is gone.

"I sometimes miss my own daughter," she says, suddenly releasing me, getting up from the table.

Right after, Jimmy's grandfather appears. And then Jimmy.

"There you are," Grandma Lilja declares, pulling a tissue from the inside of her pink sleeve, dabbing her eyes.

Grandpa Baldur smiles at her, then frowns, goes to her, kisses her deeply right on the mouth. I shake my head, smiling, and turn my eyes away.

Jimmy puts on his jacket, gets mine and pulls me out into the morning air.

"Was she talking," he asks, "about my mom?"

We're walking aimlessly down his street, the morning sun warm on our shoulders.

"She said she misses her. But she seemed really upset."

Jimmy stops. Kicks at a round stone that is burgundy red with a bolt of green lightning running through its centre.

"My mother," he says slowly, "is a schizophrenic. It's been hard on everybody."

I don't know what to say. I take his hand, thread my fingers through his as we start walking again.

"I thought you went to visit her," I say. "She lives in the city, right?"

"We *all* go to visit her. I go by myself a couple of times a year. I love her — we all do — but it just gets complicated."

I move closer. Put my arm around his waist.

"If it's any help at all, I know about complicated. Every relationship in my life is."

"Except," he says, turning to me, "for you and me. Right?"

My body still hums in remembrance of last night. It's not a question I can answer — yet.

Instead I say lightly, "I'm thinking about getting a job here — for the summer. At Isfelds, maybe."

We've reached the main drag of town with people coming and going, cars and trucks prowling Mistik Lake on their weekend rounds. Outside Isfeld's store Jimmy stops again, turns me around and pulls me into his arms.

"That would be so awesome," he says. "To have you here all summer. But…"

I pull back, surprised. "What?"

He does the thing my dad does. Looks away. Clams up. Not going to tell me what he's thinking. With a frown, he finally says, "Working for Gerald?"

"Well, who else would I work for?" I say, relieved it isn't about me. "There isn't much choice here. Besides, I kind of know him and he was nice to me when I was a kid. He might just go for it so what's the harm in asking?"

"You're absolutely right." He puts his hand on my back, guiding us both through the door. "Let's just go and do it."

~~~

We walk down the canned-goods aisle to the meat counter. Mr. Isfeld, in a white apron, glasses tipped to the end of his nose, comes out of the walk-in fridge, the leg of some animal gripped firmly in his arms. He looks startled, almost alarmed, that we are here.

"Jimmy," he says. And, "Girl."

He sets the leg on the butcher block. Wiping his hands on his apron, he comes out from behind the meat counter and over to us.

Jimmy says, "Odella wants to talk to you."

"Oh?" Mr. Isfeld pushes his glasses back up his nose. Puts a hand on his hip. "What's this about?"

"Hi," I say. "It's nothing earth-shattering."

He looks away, wipes a hand across his forehead and looks back at me with a tense smile.

I launch in. "First of all...I want to thank you for...the nice things you said about my mother in the paper." I'm stammering now, feeling like an idiot. "It's good somebody from here wrote about her. We just put it in the city paper and didn't think about Mistik Lake. It's so nice that you did that. It meant a lot — to me."

"Well, well," he says, looking like I've given him too much information. "Well," he says again.

He reaches out then, his hand rough and warm, encasing mine — shaking it firmly for a long time as if he is overcome by an emotion he doesn't know what to do with. I wonder when he'll quit.

"So I've got all this meat to cut," he murmurs and abruptly drops my hand.

Jimmy stands there the whole time looking as uncomfortable as Mr. Isfeld — arms folded tightly across his chest, hands wedged under his armpits.

I take a deep breath. "I was wondering if you could give me a job this summer."

"A...what?"

"I'm thinking about staying at the cottage for the summer. I need a job and I know that you hire locally but if you could just see a way to considering me, then..."

"Does your father know about this?"

He has reeled back against the meat counter, almost losing his balance. He catches the edge with his hand, quickly recovering himself.

"Well, yes and no," I say. "I told him I wanted to get a job and he said there weren't many opportunities…"

"Did you tell him you want to work for me?"

I look him right in the eye. "If I can find a job I can stay for the summer."

"You're sure about this."

"I want to work for you, Mr. Isfeld."

He turns away. Rearranges the packages of fresh chicken breasts. Puts the pork chops beside the sausages.

I wait. It seems he's forgotten that I'm standing there. He moves down to the steaks. Lifts them as if counting how many there are. Sets them down again. Sniffs. Wipes his nose. I wait some more.

Just when I'm starting to think we should leave, Mr. Isfeld turns around again, takes off his glasses and wipes his eyes. "Boy, it sure is hot in here. We need to open that back door. This wouldn't be a good place for a city girl to work."

"I beg your pardon?"

"There's all this, this — *meat*," he emphasizes. "I need help on meat this summer. You wouldn't be on cash. You'd be back here with me. On the meat. Not a job for a girl such as yourself. Messy work. Messy, messy work, and I only pay minimum wage. I don't think you want to work for me. I don't think you really want to work with meat."

Why is he going on and on about meat?

"Yes, I do. I do, Mr. Isfeld."

A pause.

"So that's the way it's going to be, then," he says softly.

I wait, hoping, while he thinks some more.

"All right," he says. "All right."

"I'm hired?"

He glares at me. "Don't it look that way, girl? Didn't I just say so?"

"Oh, *thank you*, Mr. Isfeld!"

"Save your thank-you. You won't feel that way come the end of summer. I got meat to cut here," he says, turning away. "When can you start?"

"School for me is finished by the May long weekend," I respond.

He stares at me, so I continue, "It's a program for advanced students. We're done early."

"I know about it," he says. "You don't have to explain it to me. One of the smart ones, are you?"

I don't know whether it's to my advantage to say yes or no. So I don't say anything.

"Okay," he says. "Report to me May long weekend. And don't be wearing fancy clothes. This is man's work — not meant for a skinny girl like you. I must have rocks in my head."

~~~

"We didn't visit enough," Grandpa Baldur says after I thank them over and over again for the weekend. "But you'll be back."

He hugs me and I hug him back, and then Grandma Lilja hugs me and says, "We'll see you again. Soon."

Jimmy follows me out to the car, puts my bag in the back seat, hunkers down by the open door as I get inside. I watch his lips, so familiar to me now, the little golden hairs surrounding them, the soft dryness of them, the heat I know I'll find there.

"I'll miss you," he whispers.

"And I'll miss you," I whisper back.

He reaches inside the car, puts his hand at the back of my neck and pulls me towards him, and I'm practically sliding off the seat.

Two and a half weeks seems like a very long time not to see him. I bury my face in his neck. He rocks me back and forth.

"I'll call you," he says at last.

I pull back to look at him.

"You are the best thing in my life, *ever* — do you know that?" he says solemnly.

I wipe my eyes. I don't know what to say. He stands and we close the door between us.

"Buckle up," he says, leaning in the open window to kiss me one more time. My heart aches with a fullness that I've never felt before.

He stands back. I catch a glimpse of his grandmother at the window, waving to me. His grandfather appears behind her, arm raised, too. I wave gaily and head for the highway.

All the way home I think about Jimmy. I think about his grandparents. I listen to sappy songs on the radio and cry. The sunset is extraordinary. The clouds are fabulous. And even though I'm not exactly sure that I want to package dead animal parts all summer, I can't wait to get back to Mistik Lake.

I finally pull into our driveway. It's late Sunday evening and I was supposed to be home hours ago. I find Sarah and Janelle in the living room watching TV, put down my things and slide in between them. Janelle lifts her feet, drops them again in my lap. Sarah lifts my arm and shoves her head under it, leaning against me. She puts her ear against my chest, listens.

"Your heart's going bumpety-bump," she says with a smile.

I kiss her hair, hug her close — warm and sweet.

Janelle snuggles her feet further into my lap, turns sideways, sticks a sofa cushion under her head. She wants me to play with her feet, so I do.

Sister sandwich, on the sofa.

After about five minutes, Dad comes into the living room, places his hands on the back of the sofa — watches us watching TV.

Then, "Did you have a good weekend?"

He sounds a bit cool, a bit testy.

"I'm sorry I'm late, Dad."

Janelle looks at him, at me, back at the TV and says, "Don't be mad at her. She wasn't *that* late."

"I'm not angry, Janelle. I'm concerned, that's all."

"Same thing," says Sarah. "She was just having a nice weekend with her boyfriend, for heaven's sake."

Dad pushes back slightly, leaving his hands on the sofa. I can feel him back there worrying, outnumbered.

Finally, "Odella, can I have a word with you, privately?"

"I have to talk to you, too," I say, moving my sisters, getting off the sofa.

I follow him into his study. He reaches around behind me and shuts the door, places a hand on my back and steers me over to the couch. I sit down at one end, he sits at the other.

Elbow resting on the back of the couch, head resting on his hand, he frowns at me in his concerned yet pissed-off way.

I think back to an early memory of Dad and me when I was very small, just before Janelle was born. Of feeling like I was on top of the world as I sat on his shoulders, his hands on my legs to steady me. I wore white stockings. And little black shoes. We stood before the long mirror in our front hall, admiring how we looked. I played with his pale hair, crunching it between my fingers. My own dark hair cascaded in waves around my face.

"Pretty girl," he said to my reflection in the mirror.

"Pretty girl," I said to his reflection.

He laughed and then repeated "Pretty girl" to the photograph hanging beside the mirror of Mom when she was two, out skating with Auntie Gloria on Mistik Lake.

Now Dad waits for me to begin our discussion. I open it by telling him something I think he'll like to hear.

"I'm not going out to Mistik Lake for a couple of weeks. Jimmy's not coming here, either. I'm going to focus on school. After that, classes will be over for us. Jimmy will have everything finished around the same time as me. He's smart, Dad. He doesn't have a single exam to write."

"I see." His mouth draws into a tight line. "Odella, I'm worried about you."

"Why?"

"I didn't like that last one you were with. Now it's starting again. Aren't you getting in over your head with this boy?"

"Yes, but not in a bad way. He's…very…wonderful."

Dad gives me a small smile. "He *is* an impressive kid — bright, as you say, and pretty mature. How old is he?"

"Eighteen. Same age as his grandfather's truck."

For some reason that makes him smile. He settles into the sofa in a more relaxed way. Waits for me to go on. Glances over at the photo on his desk of all of us, a family portrait taken just before our last Christmas together. A rare thing — Mom is in the picture because someone else took it. We are all smiling except for Sarah, who has been crying because the thing that she'd wanted to wear had chocolate milk stains all down the front. But it's a photo of us when things were kind of normal. Mom is sober in the photograph, her smile frantically cheerful. She looks a little crazy, truth be told. Dad just looks tired. Janelle has her head against Mom's arm in a clingy way. Sarah is sitting on my lap, and I remember how she rocked back and forth, bony little bum digging into my legs, until I told her to stop it right now and the photographer took the only picture of us that was worth framing.

"I went to see Mr. Isfeld on Saturday," I tell Dad at last. "I asked him to give me a summer job. He's agreed to hire me."

PART 3 *SUMMER*

– 15 –

DEALING WITH DANIEL

GLORIA

She and Kathleen are in bed. It's Sunday evening. They like to retire early and lie together in their big bed, propped against pillows, sometimes sharing a bowl of fruit and a plate of crackers. They read — sometimes alone, sometimes to each other — little snippets of things that they find funny or provocative. Sometimes they watch television — maybe the late-night news. After that they turn off the light and reach for each other in the darkness, a kiss, a cuddle, sometimes more. Almost always, one will whisper I love you. And the other whispers I love you, and then Kathleen's arm rides along her back, resting there until they fall asleep.

His call, as she's nodding off watching the national news, her head on Kathleen's shoulder, jars her out of her delicious torpor.

Daniel. Sally's Daniel.

She sits up straight and brushes cracker crumbs from her chest.

"Daniel? What on earth…"

"I'm sorry to call you so late. My God, you were probably sleeping, and I know it's been a while since we talked. I'm in trouble here, Gloria. I've got nobody to talk to about this. All hell has broken loose around here."

"Tell me about it," she says, coming fully awake.

Kathleen stirs beside her, eyelids fluttering from halfclosed to an open full question. Gloria shakes her head and mouths, "Daniel."

Kathleen sits straight up, too, watching this conversation as it unfolds.

"Can you and Kathleen come sooner than August?" he says. "Maybe come for the whole summer? I hate to ask you this. But Odella's gone crazy. She's taken it into her head to go to your cottage. Stay out there all summer. She's hooked up with a local boy. You know his grandfather, Baldur."

"Baldur? Baldur Tomasson?"

"Yes. And that boy will be over there all summer at your place shacked up with her. Worse still, she's gotten herself a job working for Gerald Isfeld." He stops briefly, then continues in a torrent, "I don't usually beg, Gloria. I find it pretty undignified at best. But you have to admit that there is potential here for a goddamn calamity."

There is a pause. She wonders if she's really up to this. The whole thing seems exhausting.

Kathleen watches steadily, understanding that something difficult is being asked, a fierce protective line forming between her brows.

"I guess I owe you this," Gloria says, locking eyes with her. "We'll come."

"Oh, God, thank you," says Daniel. "I can't thank you enough."

"Don't thank me just yet," she says. "There are certain — conditions."

Silence again.

"I know what they are," he manages. "And I hope it doesn't kill me. Kill us all."

BETWIXT AND BETWEEN

ODELLA

Dad comes to me with a haggard smile a week after our conversation in his study. He looks as if he's ready to cry.

"You can go," he says, fidgeting around, lightly slapping his hand along the kitchen counter. "And by the way, Gloria and Kathleen have decided to come a little early."

"That's fine, Dad," I say, relieved. "How early?"

"They haven't given me a definite date yet. They'll let me know."

Okay, he's hiding something. I also realize it's depressing for him — adjusting to the fact that I'm growing up.

Unfortunately, Janelle somehow finds out, before I can tell her, that I'll be at Mistik Lake all summer.

She comes out of the shower, her hair hanging in glistening strings around her eyes and asks accusingly, "So what did Dad actually say?"

"He's not happy, Janelle. He's going to let me do it anyway."

I examine my lips in the bathroom mirror, wipe off my lipgloss, reapply with lipstick.

"Right," she says, glaring at me. "You ask for the moon and he gives in to you. Anything you want."

"You'll all come out on the weekends."

Janelle pulls on a T-shirt and underpants, whips a white towel off the rack and starts to wipe blood off her leg. She's cut herself shaving with a pink disposable razor.

"You," she mutters, "are his *undeniable* favourite."

Then I say it, the thing that's going on between us that isn't about Dad.

"I'll go sometime," I tell her. "You and I both know that. I'll go — not for just a couple of months — but really actually leave home. I'll leave you alone with Sarah and Dad. Next thing, you'll go and leave Sarah and Dad rattling around in the house. After that it'll be Sarah's turn to leave. And Dad will be all by himself."

She throws the towel on the floor, sits heavily down on it.

I slide down to the floor as well. We are both in bare feet. I put my toes against her toes. Then she puts her feet against my feet, like one of us is on the other side of a mirror. We can do this because our feet are exactly the same size.

She wipes her nose. Looks at our joined feet.

"I'll *always* come back, Janelle," I say.

"Promise? Pinkie swear?" she says, like her heart is breaking.

~~~

On my way out the door I meet Sarah coming from the kitchen, a smear of sugary goo on her face and a bowl of cereal in her hand. She wraps her free arm around me and presses her face into my clean top, then pulls away, giving me a bright sticky smile. "Janelle says we're going to the lake."

"Why did she tell you such a thing?" I slip on my sandals. "It's just me going, Sarah. I've got a summer job there."

I watch her face finally register this. Wonder. Disappointment. Disbelief. Then complete and utter misery. Only a nine-year-old sister can show you such a range of emotions in the space of about ten seconds.

"Why?" she wails.

"Because it's something I have to do."

She follows me barefoot outside onto the sun-warmed cement.

It is mid-May. I'm registered at the University of Winnipeg for the fall. I'll write one final exam next week, hand in a couple of essays and I'm done. There's graduation in June, but nothing else to think about except Jimmy Tomasson and Mistik Lake all summer long. I open the car door and get inside.

"Don't you want to spend the summer with us?"

"You can call me whenever you want. You'll come out with Dad and Janelle and visit me practically every weekend. And Auntie Gloria will be here with Kathleen, and you'll all come out to the lake for a while."

She sticks her face through the open window. "Why couldn't Janelle and I just come and stay with you all summer? We wouldn't be any trouble. I promise."

I kiss her forehead. "That wouldn't work," I say, and start the car. "Watch your head."

I roll down the driveway as she shouts, "Is that your final answer?"

Before I pull onto the street, though, I catch a glimpse in the driver's mirror of what she does next. She turns and skips! Actually *skips* towards the front door!

After that I go to the mall. I promised Dad I'd pick up a few things, and there's also stuff I'll need for work at Mr. Isfeld's — extra jeans, shorts, a couple of tops — nothing, as he instructed, fancy. Also, I need a new bathing suit to replace the one I was wearing last year, which snapped a strap and couldn't be fixed.

In a little store halfway down the mall, I find a bikini with ties at the hips. It has a snaky, goddessy look and is a light coffee tone. I think about this for a moment, looking at my reflection in the dressing-room mirror, seeing my nipples rise against the silky material.

I'm happy as the salesgirl rings up the suit and I pay for it. I go back into the mall — to the elevator music being pumped through the place and the fake trees, the passing boys who smell like they've raided the men's cologne department, and groups of frantically hormonal girls with vapid smiles and over-processed hair.

Who do I see walking towards me but Derrick — alone, fumbling through his pockets like he's lost something, hair falling over his face.

I want to turn around and walk the other way.

It's too late.

His whole body registers a jolt of surprise at seeing me.

"Hi!" he says.

"I've been shopping," I tell him.

"Yeah?"

He regards me solemnly for a moment, suddenly puts his arms around me, right there in the mall, and pulls me into a tight hug.

Well, I think, he's feeling bad about everything. Why shouldn't I just hug him, too. So I do, and give him a nice friendly and extremely platonic pat on the back. It all feels pretty good. My heart is full of kindness.

Derrick's speaking, whispering something. I focus, catch these unbelievable words: "Want to go back to my place?"

I pull away. "Derrick, what the hell! No!"

He actually blushes. I fold my arms tightly across my chest and study him. As far as I know he's still with Sandy.

"I'm completely not interested in you," I finally tell him. "I can't even begin to tell you how not interested I am. But here's the thing. You aren't even subtle about being a cheating asshole."

"Everybody cheats," he says, acting like I've just handed him a compliment. "Why hide it?"

I look all around me for an escape. There is none. So I look directly at him again and laugh. I walk away laughing. It's just too bizarre.

"Oh, grow up, Odella!" I hear him call through the din of the mall as I keep on laughing.

~~~

Some days are crazy, and they just keep on getting crazier. When I arrive home, Dad's whisking a couple of glasses off the kitchen table. One clearly has lipstick marks along the rim.

He notices me noticing this and explains sheepishly, "Somebody from work. She just dropped off a project. She stayed for a drink."

Vodka spritzers in the middle of the afternoon, and the whole place smells of perfume.

"Dad," I say levelly, "there's no need to explain. If she's that hot, just go for it."

He gives me a surprised smile, looks at his feet and then back at me. Shakes his head. Is about to say something. Instead, smiles again — this time in huge amusement.

"What? What's so funny?"

He leans forward, kisses my forehead.

"You," he says, looking at me. He suddenly tears up.

I add emphatically, "In fact, I really think you need to get laid. It's about goddamn time."

He laughs out loud. It's good to hear him laugh. "I'll take that on advisement, Miss Lonelyhearts."

I leave the kitchen, humming. Stop by the mail that's piled up in the front hall.

Near the bottom is a postcard. On the front is a copy of some artist's painting — cobalt blue, purple, with streaks of brilliant green and a spider web of yellow at the left-hand corner. I turn it over. The stamps are from Iceland. No return address. The place where you'd normally write a message is pretty much covered. *List án landamæra*, it says at the top, followed by two columns of dates with people's names.

Art shows would be my guess. In what little space remains at the bottom, handwritten in black felt marker: *See you this summer!*

Unsigned, but I recognize Einar's handwriting — the long angular slope is unmistakable.

See you this summer!

Am I supposed to be overjoyed by this? Is he really coming from Iceland to see us?

− 17 −

LIFE BEYOND
HIGH SCHOOL

JIMMY

He didn't tell her what the fish said to him when he was twelve years old. He didn't actually know, recognizing it only as Icelandic — a language his grandparents spoke and, except for a few phases, he didn't understand. The words didn't matter, anyway. It was what he saw when the fish spoke. He remembers the eye filled with seductive blue luminosity. The slender naked girl with the long raven hair like Odella's. Swimming in the centre of its eye. Swimming like an incredible silky goddess. The immense eye of the fish was awesome and terrifying, the girl absolutely thrilling.

He parks in front of the *Herald*. Three more days, and then they'll have the whole summer to be together. The thought of it is beyond wonderful. He waits until he calms down before getting out of the truck.

~~~

"What are you doing this summer?" Uncle Karl asks with a frown.

"Working at Tempo, pumping gas. Start this weekend. Why?"

"And you've got that McLean girl coming out here. Staying all summer. You still going to need gas money?"

He smiles at his worried uncle, stuck in a cast that doesn't come off for another three weeks.

"Tell you what," says Jimmy. "I'm not planning on letting you down anytime soon. And that fortune you'll continue to pay me — twenty bucks here, twenty bucks there — you can think of as an investment in my future."

Uncle Karl mops his face with his hand and says, relieved, "If you ever need a reference, I'll give you the best one I could give anybody. Hell, maybe we should think of this as kind of an internship, like they do in the city. You want to be a newspaperman?"

"Absolutely."

"You have the talent for it — and the brains. Weren't you in the Advance Placement program this year?"

"That's right."

"So why aren't you doing something about it? Why don't you, for instance, register for the journalism program at Red River Community College?"

Uncle Karl's a mind reader. Still, Jimmy hesitates before he says, "I've looked into it. Tuition is really steep. Steeper than I thought. I'm looking into student loans."

"Forget that route. I'll lend you the money, interest free," says Karl. "And I won't take no for an answer. Got a nest egg for emergencies like this. Don't look so damned surprised. Think of it as a further investment in your future."

As Grandma Lilja says about the gifts that life gives you, "Pay attention." Because, of course, every gift comes with its own set of complexities — he knows this. Like the gift of living all these years with his adoring grandparents while his mother struggles alone in the dark waters of mental illness. Or his uncle now offering to give him a future while his own is tied up in a business that never quite succeeds.

— 18 —

GETTING TO KNOW
MR. ISFELD

ODELLA

Saturday morning, my first day at Isfeld's, we're in the back, just the two of us. He's showing me how to package meat. I'm trying to follow his instructions and block out the grossness I feel at picking up cold, pale bloody pork while wearing disposable gloves.

"Okay, girl," Mr. Isfeld says after a few minutes of this. "I got steaks to cut and you got to be on your own with these chops now. You got to get used to all of this."

I feel queasy, but nod in agreement.

"That's right," he offers almost encouragingly. "And by the way, if you're wondering why I wrote that piece about your mother, it's because she was a nice lady, that's all."

I'm surprised — this talk of my mother coming as it does right out of the blue — but I don't say anything.

He stands there looking at me over his glasses. The lenses are smeared with something. Whatever that something is I don't want to know.

I turn back to the pork, struggle with the plastic wrap, which comes off the roll in shreds and sticks together. I tear off another piece, which does the same thing.

Mr. Isfeld suddenly says, "Come on out the back door for a minute."

I follow him outside, wondering what's up.

"See that tree over there? Big willow?"

I do. Immense thick branches with long trailing tendrils.

"First time I remember seeing your mother, it was after I moved in with my grandfather, who owned this place. She's sitting up in that branch there — laughing at me. Fifteen years old, she was. That was the summer before…" He gives me a quick look and glances away.

"The accident? You can say it, Mr. Isfeld."

I wonder how old he was when she was fifteen.

"Well," he says distractedly, "that's it. That's all I wanted to show you. I'll bet you never knew she could be playful like that."

I feel a lump in my throat. When did that incandescent quality in Mom — that Dad described — go out?

Mr. Isfeld abruptly leaves, disappears inside his store. I look at the tree, at the way its newly greening tendrils sway in the wind. Then I go back inside, too. The pork is waiting.

~~~

A couple of times a day Jimmy finds me at the back of the store. He smiles at me like I'm the only person in the world. A flame dances up inside my heart. He brings little gifts —

coffee, muffins, lunch, his jacket on day two because it's raining and cold outside and just as cold inside in the meat section. All day long I hug it around me and it smells of him and I can hardly wait to be with him again.

On day three he sails in bringing me three orange tulips from Grandma Lilja's garden, says, "I'm making you dinner tonight," and disappears out the door again.

I'm still holding the beautiful tulips, wondering where to put them, when Mr. Isfeld, at the sink washing up, blood flowing into the basin, says, "He spending lots of time with you over at the cabin?"

I reply with a little smile, "You want me to do something with these chicken ends?"

"Package 'em, price 'em, put 'em in the freezer," he instructs tersely.

~~~

On Wednesday Mr. Isfeld asks, "You having lunch with our Mr. Tomasson?"

I'm packaging sausages. Mr. Isfeld makes them himself. They look like intestines and are a terrible grey colour. I don't like to think about what's in them. I will probably never eat another sausage again in my life.

"I'm really not that hungry," I tell him.

"Got a couple of sandwiches with our names on them," he says, hovering by my shoulder, inspecting my work. "We'll go sit under the tree. Talk about life."

"About *life*?"

He scowls, pulls off his glasses, wipes the lenses on his

apron but it makes no difference. He waves them around and says, "Find out what you're planning to do with yourself once summer is over, besides making Jimmy Tomasson the happiest boy in the world."

"Oh, that," I say.

He cracks a smile. I'm starting, in a weird way, to like him.

At noon we sit under the tree. A fragrant wind blows up the back street from Mistik Lake and there's a bird on the branch above us making a song like bubbling water.

Mr. Isfeld says, "I like orioles. They improve on nature."

I shake my head at this poetic outburst. Unwrap my sandwich. Take a bite.

"I'm in love with a wonderful woman," he admits, sighing into his own sandwich.

"Tell me about her. This is really good by the way."

"She made it for you," he says. "She's a busy woman. And I live with her. Teacher. Three beautiful kids. They call me Dad."

"That's really nice," I respond, making conversation.

He takes another bite of his sandwich, slowly chews. The bird is singing up a storm above us. Just going nuts with song, and all the time the wind's rustling and rattling the leaves.

"I'm not here to talk about me," he says. "I want to know what you're doing next year."

"Going to University of Winnipeg. Taking general arts."

"And what are you going to do with that?" He takes a long pull of his drink, sets the can in the grass beside him.

"Don't know," I say. "Maybe, eventually, I'll become a teacher."

He nods, turns up his head and watches the bird.

"No rush yet," he says, looking back at me, "to have it all figured out. There's more important things."

"Like?"

"Enjoy being young — it only comes by once."

I wait for him to elaborate on this. But he doesn't.

~~~

I come home to discover Sarah has left three messages on the machine. I try calling back. Nobody's ever there. I'm starting to miss everybody. I've never been away from them for this long before. I worry how they are getting along without me. How Dad is managing.

Later Janelle calls while I'm waiting for Jimmy.

"How do you make Mom's rosemary chicken?" she asks. "I can't find the recipe."

"It's in the cupboard over the sink. In a little brown box."

"I can't see it," she says. "Oh, wait. Is this it? Mom's handwriting? Chicken with *lemons*?"

"And rosemary. How are things?"

"Fine! I have to go."

"What have you been up to?"

"Do you wash the chicken first?"

"Yes. How's Sarah?"

"Fine. Right, it has rosemary. I have to go now. Bye."

She's gone. Not needing me a second longer.

~~~

Early Thursday morning at the cottage, with the sun

streaming through the window, Jimmy and I are tangled up together, the bed frazzled and dishevelled from our sweat and sex and carrying on. He is sleeping peacefully at the moment, eyelids damp, body still. I love looking at him. I love the smell and feel of him.

But as I lie there, the shipwrecked feeling of my sisters and me being with our mother years ago in the next room comes creeping in. I feel lonely. I want him to wake up.

He does. Fully awake, eyes startled. He raises himself on one arm, hovers over me.

"What's up?" he whispers.

"Nothing."

"Can't be nothing. What's wrong?"

He lies back down and lifts me up, settling me naked on top of him full length along his body, stroking me all along my skin. I feel a little shift as he pulls the covers up over us again, and I lay my face on his chest.

I melt against him and wonder how anybody could get tired of this, this skin-to-skin closeness of being with the one person who means so much to you.

"Odella? What's wrong?"

Because he seems to need an answer I tell him the less complicated one. "Sometimes — I miss everybody."

His body has gone very still. "I guess you're lucky that way."

I raise my head, look at him in astonishment.

He stares at the ceiling. "You have your dad and two sisters. They'll all be around for a long time. I have my grandparents who won't be. And an uncle who is a great guy but he's got his own issues. And, yeah, my mom, who is not exactly what you'd call a safe harbour. I used to worry about being alone. About ending up alone."

He's gone all cold and hurt and sad on me. He'll probably get up off this bed next thing. Before I know it, before I have a chance to think about all this, he'll be putting on his clothes, walking out the door.

Instead he pulls me against him again and says into my hair, "And now you show up. You're in my heart, Odella. And even though you won't say it, I think maybe I'm in yours."

I can't tell him — yet. So I hold him as tight as I can, hoping that that's answer enough for now.

~~~

Near the end of the day, my last working day of the week, I help Mr. Isfeld put steaks on little white trays and wrap them in plastic and price them for the summer people who, he says, will trickle in before the weekend rush, looking for something to barbecue. I can't believe how much meat he sells in such a small town and I tell him this.

"There are a couple of thousand cottages, approximately, all around the lake," he responds. "Do my best business starting right now and all through the summer. Before I met Connie I used to go away for a while in the winter. Visit my mother in Toronto. But Mom had a stroke last fall and I brought her back here to live at the seniors' home. And of course Connie's busy teaching and her kids are all at school."

"My aunt Gloria lives in Toronto," I tell him. "She's coming to visit sometime this summer."

"Gloria," he says, and presses his lips together in a tight line.

"Do you know her?"

"Yep, I know your aunt. She hasn't been here for a lot of years."

"That's right," I say. "She pretty much gave the family cottage to Mom."

Mr. Isfeld disappears inside the walk-in fridge. Several minutes later he comes back empty-handed. I have arranged the steaks decoratively in the display case.

He stands and looks at them for several seconds before he says, "Put them back the way they were. We're selling meat here, girl. People don't like it when you fancy it up on them."

"But it's boring."

"It's meat, Odella. Meat is all it is. People want to see the price. Everything's got to be out in the open. No tricks."

"Okay, okay, I'll put it back the way it was. But it's still boring."

As I'm fixing them again, an elderly woman with a walker and a string bag comes clumping up to the display case.

"Afternoon, Gerald," she says, and nods at me.

"Can I help you?" I say.

She scowls. "I can help myself."

"Annie," says Mr. Isfeld, "how's that back of yours?"

"Piss poor," she says, rummaging through all the steaks, finally reaching painfully past them to choose a small package of chicken wings.

"Those are on sale," Mr. Isfeld tells her.

"I hope they're fresh," she says to him. And to me, "I

heard you were working for Gerald. Sorry to hear about your mother."

"Thanks." I don't know her and I don't know what else to say.

She turns back to Mr. Isfeld and says, "Nice you got her working for you, Gerald. Hope her father doesn't mind."

Mr. Isfeld responds without enthusiasm, "Good seeing you, Annie."

After she leaves, I say, "What was that all about?"

He picks up a knife, starts sharpening it, thinks about this and then says, "Let's take a break."

The green behind his store is becoming familiar to me. We go out there and I'm startled to see him take a thin cigar from his pocket and light it.

"I didn't know you smoked."

He blows away a thin trail of smoke. "I don't. Just once in a while. Used to smoke all the time when I knew your mother."

Then, abruptly, he adds, "I used to date her. That's all Annie meant."

"You dated my mother?"

"Long time ago. She was about a year older than you are now. I was twenty-seven at the time. Too old for her, I guess."

He takes another drag on his cigar. His hand is trembling. He slowly releases the smoke.

I think about the obituary that he wrote. I can't believe this conversation is happening.

"How long" — I hesitate — "did you date her?"

I wait some more. Finally look at him. A tear has trickled down one side of his face.

"You don't have to talk about this, Mr. Isfeld. Really, you don't."

"Yeah," he says, speaking softly, "yeah, I do. There's something you need to know about her. It might help you to understand her a little better. But first things first. Summer before she turned nineteen I'm down by the beach one night. It's the middle of July, a real hot night around ten o'clock. I'm sitting on the hood of the old man's car, minding my own business, drinking a beer, when your mother arrives, walks past me, dives into the water and takes a swim. Nobody around but the two of us."

He pauses, takes out another cigar and lights it. "She was so pretty. I never missed the opportunity of just looking at her, but I swear to you that that was all I'd ever hoped for. Well, she comes out of the water, all dripping wet and shivering, hasn't even brought a towel with her, comes over to the car and gets up on the hood bold as anything, right beside me. Asks for a beer and a cigarette. I give her both and that's when it starts."

He slowly exhales and shakes his head. "Nobody had to tell me to feel bad for robbing the cradle — but it didn't seem to bother her. We started dating. Spent a lot of time together that summer. So here's the thing you need to know: one time, we're parked up on a hill looking down at Mistik Lake and she says, 'That night, the night of the accident? I'm responsible for everyone being out on the ice. It was a dare, a stupid dare. Gordon MacDonald was driving, but I was the one who put him up to it, who dared him to do it.'"

"A *dare?*"

"That's right. I never told anybody about this, and I really don't think she told anyone else — not even your dad. She was so impressed with him. She thought that he would hate her. I bet he wouldn't have. You have to understand that vehicles *still* drive out on Mistik Lake in winter. Done it myself. You got to be careful — can't go roaring around at midnight and, most of all, there's certain spots on the ice you have to avoid. And she was just a kid, Odella. Kids do dumb things on a dare. Most of the time they get away with it."

"But *she* didn't," I say, feeling horrified for my mother, and sad, and yet — he's right, it explains things. The fact that she'd never gotten over it — and the various really wrong ways in which she'd tried.

"Nobody has to follow a dare — to go along with it — but the problem was your mother had built it up in her mind and locked it away. It was eating her up, you could tell. Secrets have a way of doing that."

~~~

"When are your dad and sisters getting here?" Jimmy asks later, when I call him at the Tempo station. The nights he pumps gas he goes directly there from helping his uncle at the *Herald*. He starts his shift around the time I finish mine.

"Sometime tomorrow," I tell him. "I'm not exactly sure when because Dad might take the day off."

"I want us to go to the boathouse tonight," Jimmy says.

"Okay. I have something to tell you."

I get off the phone and clean up the cottage so it doesn't

look as if he's been living here with me. Then I mow the lawn. I think about Mom. I try to imagine myself in her position — lonely, scared, carrying around a secret that I've never told anyone. Then I tell someone who won't judge me. I meet someone else and marry him. But every summer I come face to face with the keeper of my secret. It's in every glance he gives me. In every little gift he gives to my daughters. In every package of meat he carefully wraps and hands to me. It's there every time when with the nod of my head I say, I see you, you cared about me once and you have my secret.

~~~

At the boathouse the lake slips darkly over the rocks, a half-moon sits in the deep blue of the northern night, and stars are just beginning to show. Jimmy is building a fire on the beach. He's brought a pizza and cans of iced tea. It's an unseasonably warm night.

"Hi," he says, coming away from the fire, putting his arms around me. "Happy anniversary — it's been six weeks. Sorry I was hard on you about your family this morning."

"It's okay. I have to find a way to stop being so fixated on them. I will, somehow. I haven't eaten yet — let's eat something, I'm starving."

Halfway through the first slice of pizza, though, I lose my appetite.

"I learned something today," I say. "About my mom. And I need to tell you."

"Okay. Sounds serious."

Jimmy, who can eat an amazing amount no matter what, goes through three slices, listening hard to my story, staring into the fire.

"Heavy stuff, Odella," he says at last. "I don't know what to say. Except Gerald's right about people on the ice. My friend Grant and I used to do some pretty stupid shit out there, too — on his snowmobile. And yeah, we got away with it, but I can't imagine if we hadn't."

"Worse thing was she felt totally to blame, but kept it a secret." I poke at the fire with a stick. We watch the sparks dissipate in the night sky. "Sure explains her nightmares. No wonder she had them."

"I have a confession, too," Jimmy says. "I knew there'd been something pretty special between Gerald and your mother."

"You *knew*?"

"Uncle Karl told me. No details, and I didn't ask for any. Guess I didn't want to know. It was the day I tracked down copies of the piece Gerald wrote about your mom in the *Herald*. That's partly why I felt a little weirded out about you going to work for him."

I let this sink in for a minute. I think about the old woman at the meat counter, Annie, saying, *Hope her father doesn't mind.* So were Dad and Mr. Isfeld *rivals* the summer she turned nineteen?

"Dear God," I say. "I'll bet half of Mistik Lake knew."

"Hate to say it," Jimmy offers, "but while it was going on probably the whole town knew."

"I have no idea how she felt about him. He might have been in love with her, though. She made a big impact on him."

He scoots over, spreads out the blanket we've been sitting on and lies back, pulling me down into his arms.

"I have absolutely no doubt of that, either," he says. "If your mom was anything like you at that age."

– 19 –

THE TRUTH REVEALED

ODELLA

Two o'clock in the afternoon and the family pulls into the driveway. It's been raining all day and the sky is dark. Dad jumps out first, rain slicker pulled over his head, hand raised to greet me as I watch him from the screened-in breezeway. Sarah and Janelle leap out into the rain, whooping it up, and then Gloria steps out of the van clutching her rain jacket, raising her eyes to me.

What a surprise! I didn't expect her this soon. She hurries to the cottage door. Closely following her is a stocky handsome woman with white hair.

As Dad and Janelle and Sarah stand by the van unloading things, Gloria pulls off her jacket and quickly gathers me into her arms.

"We've come early, I know," she says, her flowery perfume rising from her warmth.

Before I can react, she's pulling away.

"Kathleen," she says, teary-eyed, "this is Odella."

"Good to be here," Kathleen says with a nod. "Gloria's been beside herself for about a week now. I keep telling her to quit fussing."

"Oh, Kathleen," says Gloria with an affectionate backward glance, "I've never fussed in my life."

Kathleen, hands in her pockets, strolls off into the main part of the cottage and leaves us alone together.

"I really didn't think you'd be here so soon," I tell Gloria. "Nobody told me it would be this weekend."

She holds my arm, says soothingly, "We've got some things to work out as a family. Your father and I thought that it would be best to do it now."

Dad, trailed by Janelle and Sarah, comes through the door — all three loaded down with dripping bags and parcels.

"Dad?" I say.

"Yes, honey," he says with a kind of nervous good cheer. "Let me just get settled here. Gloria, should I make some coffee?"

"It's already made," I tell him.

"How's the job going?" He picks up a blue towel that I forgot from my shower and left hanging over one of the chairs. He dries his hair with it. Looks at me.

Janelle and Sarah have gone out to the breezeway to claim a sofa and set up a board game. They'll be back before too long to raid the fridge and discover the chocolate cheesecake that I made for them this morning.

Gloria's over in the kitchen area taking cups down from the cupboard, smiling at them like they are old friends.

"Job's fine, Dad," I say, going to the fridge to get milk for the coffee.

"Mr. Isfeld treating you well?"

I pull my head from the fridge, set the milk on the counter.

"He's a good person. But you probably knew that."

Gloria and Dad exchange looks. Dad starts pouring coffee for everyone.

"I don't know him that well," he says, setting down the pot. He leans against the counter. His hands have begun to tremble.

"I like him a lot, Dad. He's honest."

I watch his face. It has drained of all its colour. He looks away as if I have just struck him, then back, his expression crumpling oddly as he slowly exhales.

It's in this look that I suddenly find the truth. And I know what they've all, until this moment, been hiding.

In a panic I think, I've got to leave, get out of here. I snatch up my bag, catch a watery glimpse of Mistik Lake past the windows as I frantically search for car keys, hand slipping past tissues and makeup tubes and slippery packages of condoms and pens. Instead I connect with a pink stone Jimmy found near the boathouse last night and gave to me because it's like a misshapen heart. I'm dizzy as I bring it into my hand and hold it tight.

Dad has taken only a few strides to reach me. Then we collapse into the armchair and he gathers me into his arms. Holds me like I'm a little kid.

"My girl," he whispers brokenly. "My baby girl."

DEALING WITH GERALD

GLORIA

Before she left for Iceland, Sally had warned Daniel, "If you ever feel you have to tell Odella, I guess that's your decision. But I'll come back and kill you, I swear, if I find out you've told her behind my back. We have to do it together."

Now the thing they all feared would happen *has* happened. Nothing more to be done except call Gerald and ask him to get over to the cottage.

"I'll be right there," he tells Gloria.

She thinks back to a cool spring morning fifteen years ago, Gerald showing up at her brownstone apartment in Toronto, waiting for her under the dripping front awning. At first she didn't recognize him — one of those tricks the mind plays when seeing somebody out of context.

"Miss Thorsteinsson," he greeted her politely, nothing like the gruff young man she remembered. He stepped up beside her almost timidly. "Remember me? It was a couple of years back. At Mistik Lake. I'm Gerald."

"Gerald — Isfeld?"

"Been down here visiting my mom," he said. "Violet."

"Violet — here in Toronto?"

"Yeah, I know — she moves around. She had your old address so I thought I'd look you up. See you're still here," he said with a small, downcast smile.

"Well, what can I do for you?"

"Can I buy you a coffee?"

They walked to a place across the street and found a table near the back. After the waitress brought them their coffee, Gerald sat for several long minutes warming his large hands around the white mug and staring at the rain through the bleary windows.

Gloria waited patiently, sipping her own coffee. Now that she was over the initial shock of seeing him, her mind flew back to a phone call from Sally three months after that weekend when everything went so wrong.

Sally in tears. "I'm pregnant, Auntie. Tell me what to do."

"You're *pregnant* — oh, Sally, you can't be."

"Gerald doesn't know and I don't want him to know. Daniel thinks it's his. But it isn't. I'm almost one hundred percent sure it's Gerald's. And don't tell me to go and get an abortion. I can't do it. I've killed enough people in my life." She began to sob.

"Dear God, Sally, how can you say such a thing? How could you even think it? *Killed* people? And *how* could you have gotten yourself into this mess?"

In the coffee shop in Toronto, Gerald sat back and struggled to express himself.

"Miss Thorsteinsson — Gloria," he began.

Gloria sat completely still and gathered herself in — masking her face as she was used to doing. This was something that had become, in so many areas of her life, a practised art.

He nervously sipped his coffee, put down the cup. "I've been thinking." He gathered his fleshy, muscular mouth into a straight line and continued, "You know that little girl that your niece gave birth to in August two and a half years ago. She might look like me — a little." He raised his eyes hopefully to meet hers.

"Oh, Gerald," she had said, letting go a breath, gathering her hands in her lap. "I don't know where you came up with this idea. Odella is Daniel's child." She leaned forward then, almost conspiratorially. "Just between you and me" — she let out a little laugh — "she's very much like him. She even has his talent for drawing things. You should see — she's really quite beyond her years, a very clever child. Of course, she gets that from Sally, too."

It was a cruel thing to say. At the time, however, it seemed to work. It seemed to convince him.

"I see," he said, struggling again for words, fingers trembling slightly against the thick mug. "I see," he said again. "I guess that's it, then."

"I'm so sorry, Gerald," she said, watching as he awkwardly got up from the table. "If there's anything I can do."

"No, there's nothing," he told her, laying, for just the span of a heartbeat, one large, broad butcher's hand at the edge of their table. And then the hand was gone and so was Gerald. Out onto the street. Back into the rain.

The problem of Gerald, of course, never went away. The following summer the letters started.

Pardon me for saying this, he wrote in one. *Sally's a depressed person — doesn't take a genius to see that — and as such she is headed for troubled waters. And she's going to take that little girl with her.*

And then, just after Odella's fourth birthday, a call from Sally — so upset that at first Gloria didn't recognize her niece's voice.

"Daniel *knows*?" said Gloria, sitting down quickly beside the phone. "Calm down, Sally. Take a breath. How?"

"Gerald called the cottage this weekend. We'd just got to the lake. Phone rings. It's him and he wants to know how I am. I tell him to leave me alone. Daniel says, 'Who is that?' And takes the phone before I can put it down. It all happened so fast that I didn't have time to prepare for it, nothing — it just came out. Honestly, I don't think Gerald was planning to say the things he did. Daniel is shattered. Poor, poor Daniel. I've lied to him, Auntie Gloria. He had a right to know that Odella wasn't his and I kept it from him. I don't think he'll ever forgive me."

She was crying again — wrenching little sobs that were like blows to Gloria's heart. This calamity that she had helped bring about by her silence. But hadn't Daniel been part of it, too? He must have known. How could he not? Any fool doing the math…

As for Gerald, he kept writing letters. Sometimes, when she'd had the heart for it, she'd answered them. Most times she hadn't.

His letters were full of remorse over what had happened. What he hadn't meant to let happen.

I just wanted, he wrote sorrowfully in one of them, *the best for that little girl. I guess it was all a mistake. I should never have interfered with that family. I see that now. I should have left well enough alone.*

~~~

And now she watches as Gerald pulls into the driveway in his black truck — parking in the clearing under the poplars with their slender, bone-white trunks swaying in the breeze. The sun has come out. Everything is dappled with light.

Gerald swings down from the cab of his truck, the years since she has seen him making him only slightly worse for wear. She steps outside the cottage door and waits for him. He moves towards her, avoiding the rivulets of water that are still coursing down the ruts in the driveway.

Reaching her, taking her outstretched hand, he shakes it and they stand this way for a moment — each trying to come upon the right words to say.

Gerald speaks first. "I'll bring a load of gravel from town. Spread it on your driveway if you like. Fill in some of these ruts." Without losing a beat, he adds, "Odella told me you'd be here sometime this summer."

"Daniel's inside with her now," Gloria tells him. "Odella knows, Gerald. Daniel and I were planning to tell her together this weekend. Unfortunately the truth came out before we got the chance."

He nods. "Want me to talk to her?"

"Yes, it's long overdue. Let's go inside. Let's see what can be done."

– 21 –

AFTERMATH

ODELLA

My sisters stand in the living room like statues in a kid's game where you aren't supposed to move.

Sarah's voice. "What's going on? What's wrong, Odella?"

And Janelle. "Did somebody die?"

"No," I manage, "it's okay. We'll all be okay. I'll tell you later."

"Why are you crying? Dad?"

Raising his cheek from my hair, he clears his throat and says, "We'll have to talk about this later, girls."

"Why later?" Sarah asks. "Why not now?'

Kathleen, to my relief, takes over. "Come on, Janelle, Sarah — let's go for a walk. Show me around this place."

"I want to know what's wrong," Sarah insists.

Janelle, still looking at me, suddenly puts her arm around our baby sister and says, "Come on, Sarah. I'll share my bubble gum with you."

"How come? You never share."

"I love bubble gum," Kathleen says as she herds them both out the door.

Seconds later, Aunt Gloria comes back with Mr. Isfeld, who looks embarrassed and a little sad. This must be a terrible joke that God is playing on me, on all of us. How can he be my actual father? But it's no joke. This is real and it's happening.

Mr. Isfeld sits in a chair near Dad and me. Sits at the edge like the chair might break. Holding a baseball cap that says *Mistik Valley Credit Union*. It's dark blue. He twists it around in his big hands. Dad and I are now sitting on the sofa, his arm around me. Mr. Isfeld looks at Dad, then at me, leans across, takes my hand, cups it and shakes it around a bit.

"How're you doing there, girl?"

"I'm okay," I say, and start crying again.

"There, there," he says, my hand still in his. "Well, it's been quite the day." He looks at Dad and back at me. "Not every day a girl finds out she's got two fathers. A main dad, like the one you've got here who's loved you to pieces all your life. And a funny old one like me — kind of a backup dad — but only, I got to add, if you ever want or need one."

This is going to take some getting used to. I don't know how I feel about anything right now.

Mr. Isfeld bows his head, raises it again, addresses Dad. "I'm real sorry about this."

"Why didn't you ever tell me?" I say to Dad, wiping my eyes with my sleeves.

Gloria rushes to the bathroom, comes back with a box of tissues, hands it over to me and joins us.

"I wouldn't have hated you," I tell Dad. "I would have understood something about my life. About Mom — maybe that's why she left us."

Mr. Isfeld releases my hand and sits back. He places his cap on his knee and slowly wipes each eye.

"She didn't leave because of you," Dad says firmly. "Don't you *ever*, for a single minute, think that. You are a blessing in this world, and so are your sisters. Your mother left us because she felt she had to. She and I were both to blame for that. There's so many things we didn't deal with and should have."

Mr. Isfeld raises his eyes to mine and I know one of us will have to tell about the dare.

But he stops me before I can, leaning forward, saying quietly, "Sally blamed herself for that accident, Daniel. Odella and I had a long talk about it yesterday."

After that, one by one, they each tell their stories — Mr. Isfeld, Gloria and Dad. The pieces start to fit. There are some surprises along the way, especially for me.

Mom was pregnant when she left for Iceland. Janelle and Sarah and I have a two-and-a-half-year-old baby sister named Marina.

"A baby?" I say. "Mom had a baby?"

"Yes," Dad says. "This was really your mother's job to tell you. Of course she never got the chance…"

It seems very hard for him to go on. After a while he manages, "It would have been so good for us all. She was coming back, you know, this summer for a visit. She'd done some thinking. Some healing. It would have been so good."

Later, as Mr. Isfeld leaves, I go out to his truck with him.

He stands by the driver's door, once again twirling his base-ball cap awkwardly in his hand. There's a line around his head where the hat has flattened his hair. I don't want him to be my father.

He says, "I'll see you at work tomorrow."

"Yeah, I'll be there." I start to cry all over again.

"I know you will. You've got guts, girl," he says. "I'm proud of you."

Then, natural as anything, he puts a bear-like arm around me, gives me a squeeze and — this is a surprise — kisses my forehead just the way Dad does.

– 22 –

A BIRTHDAY

JIMMY

On Odella's eighteenth birthday, he buys eighteen tea candles in glass votives at a summer clearance sale at Isfeld's.

Gerald cuts him a deal, knocking a further forty percent off, seeing as how it's for Odella. Coming away from his meat counter, he wraps them up for Jimmy personally — it's Odella's day off — all in tissue paper so they won't break, saying, "You going to surprise her at the boathouse?"

"Yeah," he responds. How the hell does Gerald know about the boathouse?

Gerald tucks away the last candle, lifts the bag gingerly by the handles. As he passes it over the counter, he advises, more about Odella than about the candles, "Be careful, now."

"No worries there," Jimmy assures him. "I'm in love with her."

"Good," Gerald says. "You'd better be."

~~~

Later, Odella creeps shivering into his arms, the lake breeze cool on their skin, the candles glowing all around them, and she tells him about a dream she had just last night.

"You were in it," she says, settling her back against him, spoon-fashion. "So was my mother. It was winter. We were standing on the ice and you had your arms around me and I felt safe. Mom came up to us and put her hand on my heart. It was warm — her hand, just as if she was still alive. She looked at me for a long time and I was crying and she just kept looking at me. She was saying goodbye, I know that. And I forgave her, Jimmy. When she walked away I could finally do that. But I'll never understand her. She did things that I would never ever do."

"That's because you're you," he says. "Not her."

He pulls her closer. Enfolds her as they watch a full moon rise, shimmering, over Mistik Lake.

– 23 –

A FINAL GIFT FROM ICELAND

ODELLA

Janelle and I sit out in the breezeway on a gentle day in late August. We are sharing a bowl of green grapes, and Janelle who doesn't like the skins, is meticulously peeling each one — her skinny fingers picking away. When she has three peeled she shoves everything in her mouth at once, quickly chews, swallows. I smile at this — at all this effort for a tiny moment of pleasure — and wonder if she'll still be eating grapes the same way when we get to be old ladies.

"Remember that last time we saw Mom?" says Janelle out of the blue. "We didn't know it would be the last time, did we?"

"I guess you never know," I tell her. "If you did, maybe you'd do things differently."

"She picked us up in the car, remember? And took us out for lunch and to buy some books. Tell me about that day," says Janelle. "The day we last saw her."

"Sarah wanted a book about dinosaurs. She chose five. Mom put back four. Got herself a book in the travel section about Iceland."

"And later, she drove us home and then we all sat there for a while, remember?" says Janelle. "Parked for a long time in front of the house."

"And the leaves are skittering down the street," I tell her. "It's October. And Sarah's got a death grip on Mom and Mom's saying 'I'll see you next week, Sarah.'"

"I was so mad about everything that I finally got out of the car and I didn't say goodbye and I didn't even turn around," Janelle says with a little sob. "I never even got a last look at her."

"It's okay," I say, gathering her in my arms, hugging her fiercely. "She watched you."

"She did?"

"Yes, she did," I say, finding at last the one thing that I can give my sister. "She smiled and she watched you go. She watched you walk all the way up the sidewalk. And then she didn't look away until you were safely inside."

~~~

Later that evening I come out to get some air — everyone else is inside the cottage, Jimmy trouncing them in a noisy game of Scrabble — and a beige van pulls halfway up the driveway and parks.

The driver's door opens, setting off a bell that's clear and pretty. Stepping out into the moonlight, tall and muscular, something in his build like a Viking, is Einar. He raises his large hand in greeting. I raise my hand back and watch as he goes around to the other side of the van.

He reaches inside and unbuckles a small sleepy child. He eases her up into his arms, whispers something and carefully watches her smile flower before he moves forward. She's very blonde. Little curls frame her face. He lightly tugs the hood away from the back of her head.

"Odella?" he says, coming up to me.

"Yes," I reply.

Under the light over the doorway the child gazes up at me, her eyes so much like Mom's — same colour, same shape — that it makes me catch my breath. She reaches out a small shy hand.

I take it, and then, because she smiles again, so suddenly and beautifully, I reach for her and she comes easily into my arms.

She smells sweet and fresh — carrying some magical memory of Iceland that clings to her clothes and hair.

"Hello, there," I say, while Einar looks on and watches me fall in love with her. "Oh, hello, you darling girl. Come inside, come in and meet your sisters."